"Why Do

she whispered when ... the silence.

Kirk watched the way ... tongue darted across her lips, and saw the sorrow that was filling her eyes.

"I don't hate you, Cassandra," he said, "that's my problem." He released her arm, but didn't step away.

Their eyes met again, and both Cassandra and Kirk understood what had been said, and what had not. Then Kirk, his eyes sweeping across Cassandra's face, took a single step and closed the distance between them.

MONICA BARRIE

a native of New York State, has traveled extensively around the world but has returned to settle in New York. A prolific romance writer, Monica's tightly woven emotional stories are drawn from her inherent understanding of relationships between men and women.

Dear Reader:

Romance readers have been enthusiastic about the Silhouette Special Editions for years. And that's not by accident: Special Editions were the first of their kind and continue to feature realistic stories with heightened romantic tension.

The longer stories, sophisticated style, greater sensual detail and variety that made Special Editions popular are the same elements that will make you want to read book after book.

We hope that you enjoy this Special Edition today, and will enjoy many more.

Please write to us:

Jane Nicholls
Silhouette Books
PO Box 236
Thornton Road
Croydon
Surrey CR9 3RU

MONICA BARRIE
Silken Threads

Silhouette Special Edition

Originally Published by Silhouette Books
division of
Harlequin Enterprises Ltd.

First published in Great Britain 1985
by Mills & Boon Ltd, 15–16 Brook's Mews, London W1A 1DR

© Monica Barrie 1985

Silhouette, Silhouette Special and Colophon are Trade Marks of Harlequin Enterprises B.V.

ISBN 0 373 09221 0

23-0785

Made and printed in Great Britain by
Richard Clay (The Chaucer Press) Ltd,
Bungay, Suffolk

Another Silhouette Book by Monica Barrie

Silhouette Special Edition
Cry Mercy, Cry Love

*For further information about
Silhouette Books please write to:*

Jane Nicholls
Silhouette Books
PO Box 236
Thornton Road
Croydon
Surrey CR9 3RU

Silken Threads

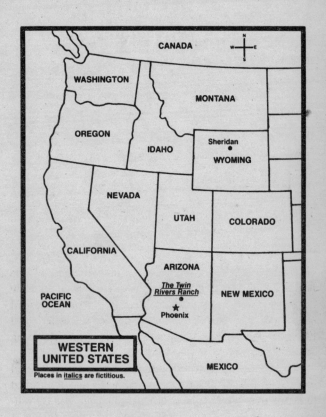

WESTERN UNITED STATES

Places in *italics* are fictitious.

Chapter One

It was an enchanting evening, perhaps one of the loveliest that Cassandra Leeds had experienced in New York. She stood on the penthouse terrace and gazed upward at the clear star-studded sky that resembled a jeweler's pad of black velvet, complete with ten-thousand sparkling diamonds strewn carelessly across it.

The moon was a small crescent off to one side, and tonight, instead of its customary yellowish tint, it gleamed almost a pure white. The cool late-winter air was refreshing, and she welcomed its caress and the goose bumps it brought out on her bared skin.

The black sleeveless Halston she wore was as dark as the heavens; her lightly tanned skin contrasted fetchingly with the silk. Her long hair was swept back, held in place by two silver hair combs, while the breeze tossed the unruly length about randomly.

Behind her, inside the penthouse, the sounds of conversation and music filtered through the closed glass doors, but she pushed them away. She did not want to be reminded of the people inside, especially of Somner.

For over a year, she and Somner Barwell had been an "item." He was pleasant enough, she thought, but he wasn't really the man she wanted to spend her life with. Cassandra didn't know what she wanted to do with the rest of her life. She was twenty-six—almost twenty-seven. With each passing year, she seemed to become more confused rather than more certain about herself.

And Somner was beginning to treat her as one of his possessions. He, like the rest of the people they knew, seemed to think it was an established fact that she and Somner would marry.

She knew Somner would be a great catch—he had all the prerequisites: he was good-looking, wealthy, and respected. Somner traveled the world and was rich enough to buy whatever he wanted. He had a large art collection, beautiful cars, summer residences in the south of France, the Hamptons, Malibu, and, of course, this home—a Fifth Avenue penthouse.

"Happy, darling?" Somner asked as he stepped out onto the terrace and came up behind her. His hands wound around her slim waist, clasping together at the very center of her stomach before gently drawing her to him.

"How could I not be?" she replied, turning slightly to glance at him from the corners of her eyes. He was handsome in a very traditional way. He wore his hair short, kept his face clean-shaven, and always smelled of aftershave. His nails were manicured and his clothing was always impeccable.

He released her and Cassandra took a deep breath.

"That makes me very happy," he said, stepping beside her. Then his hand went into his jacket pocket. "Cassandra, you already know how I feel about you." Pausing, he withdrew his hand. In it was a velvet box.

Not yet, she cried silently.

Slowly, with a smile on his mouth, Somner opened the box and, despite her trepidation, Cassandra gasped. Within the box sat a magnificent engagement ring. A large marquis-cut emerald that looked to be five carats glinted in the terrace's low light.

Before she could speak, Somner had the ring out of the box and was moving it to her hand. It was then that she forced her mind into action.

Stepping back, Cassandra shook her head slowly. "No, Somner, not yet," she whispered as she turned and ran from him. She sped through the large living room, ignoring the startled glances thrown her way.

She grabbed her small purse from where she had left it and, without even bothering with her coat, raced out of the apartment and into the waiting elevator.

Moments later she was on Fifth Avenue, waving her arm to attract a passing cab. When one stopped, she ran to it, and just as she heard Somner call her name from the door of the building, got in and closed the door.

When the cab started rolling, Cassandra breathed deeply.

"Where to?" asked the cabby as he gazed at her in his rearview mirror. His eyes took in the fact that she wore no coat and that her dress was not designed for the cold weather. He could also tell, from his years of experience, that she was one of "them"—the idle rich.

"Just drive for a few minutes, please," she whispered in a voice barely loud enough for him to hear.

The driver shrugged his shoulders and began to drive

slowly along the avenue while Cassandra tried to organize her thoughts and figure out what she should do.

A moment later a smile etched its way across her taut features. She opened her purse and glanced at the contents. Within the small black bag were her cosmetics, a small credit card case, and her passport. For some reason, Cassandra always carried her passport.

"Kennedy Airport," she told the driver.

Stepping out of the limousine, Cassandra gazed around. In the three months she had been gone, little had changed in New York. *But*, she thought with a smile, *I've changed*.

Then she walked to the entrance of the large, modern office building housing Leeds International. When she entered the lobby, she felt the first twinge of anxiety. By the time she left the elevator on the forty-seventh floor, her stomach was filling with butterflies; when she opened the door to her father's outer office, she was afraid her legs wouldn't support her.

Cassandra Leeds had good reason to be nervous. Her father was furious. He was angrier than she'd ever known him to be in her entire life.

"Good afternoon, Miss Leeds," called the receptionist. "Welcome back from Greece."

Cassandra's eyes flicked to the smiling young woman, and she wondered if the receptionist knew the story behind Cassandra's appearance here today.

"Thank you, Alice," she replied, keeping her voice calm and level.

"Go right in, your father's waiting for you."

Cassandra smiled hesitantly. "That's what I was afraid of," she said as she started toward the forbidding glass doors of her father's office.

Chapter Two

Three months! You disappear for three months as if there were nothing in the world to concern you other than a crazy whim striking you! What do you have to say for yourself?" Gregory Leeds demanded in a voice so low and angry that it sounded like a shout to Cassandra's ears.

Staring at her father, she took in his rigid features. The sharp lines of his face, which had always seemed so handsome to her, now looked foreboding in the extreme.

"I had to get away," she replied, managing to keep her voice firm when she finally spoke.

"Did you? Did you have to get away, or run away? Cassandra, you're twenty-seven years old. You have had everything you've ever asked for; and you've taken quite a few things you didn't ask for. But this irresponsibility must stop."

"I'm sorry, Father, but I had a lot on my mind. I had to

sort everything out,'' Cassandra stated, forcing herself to shed her fear of her father and stand up for herself.

Gregory Leeds stared at his daughter in disbelief. He knew, had always known, that he spoiled his daughter. He had done so from the moment she'd been born and been unable to stop himself. Once he'd learned his wife could no longer have children, he'd hoped Cassandra would take over his work. She had always been a bright, willful, headstrong child, but she had been a good child also.

Then came the riding accident, and Cassandra, who had always been fearless, changed, and for the first time in his memory, had become afraid of something. She had never been the same since.

''And have you sorted 'everything' out?'' the elder Leeds asked sarcastically.

''Yes. I realized I'm not ready for marriage yet. I need to do something for myself first,'' Cassandra told him. It was true. In the three months she had spent in Greece, she had realized that her life felt empty, that there was nothing in it that gave her any real personal satisfaction.

''And you don't consider marriage to one of the fastest-rising businessmen in the world, 'something to do for yourself'? Cassandra, having a family is very important.''

''I'm not ready to become a high-class breeder for Somner Barwell!'' Cassandra stated, growing angry at her father and losing her fear.

''Really? Well, let me tell you something, young lady. That's about all you are ready for! That's all you can do! You dropped out of college in your last semester. You've never spent a day in your life working—not even charity work like your mother. No, all you do is run around the world playing with your friends, who do as much for themselves as you do for yourself. And you have the audacity to tell me that you want to find yourself?'' Gregory Leeds had finally lost that final thread of self-control that had been so tenaciously holding his temper in check. Finally eighteen years of watching his only child waste her life had taken its toll.

''Are you saying I'm worthless?'' Cassandra asked, her mind numbed by her father's heated outburst, her cheeks flaming with both anger and humiliation.

''No, Cassandra,'' her father said in a constrained voice, ''it's only what you've been showing me and the rest of the world.'' Then Gregory Leeds made himself relax before speaking again. ''I think that a marriage between you and Somner would be for the best. You have to start living like a normal person.''

His words had the power of a hard slap, and Cassandra's mind whirled with the attack. For the last three months Cassandra had led a secluded life, staying with her oldest friend, who had a house in Greece, rarely going out in public, just spending each day in deep thought.

What bothered her most was that her father was voicing some of the very things she herself had thought about. Her anger at him was also an anger directed at herself, because, to a small degree, her father was right.

''I'm still not ready to marry Somner.''

''I'm sorry, Cassandra, but I think it would be for the best.''

A white-hot streak of irrational anger surged through her mind. She stiffened, and her hazel eyes turned as cold as her father's.

''I'm sorry, Father, but I don't. I have a life of my own, and I plan to live it!''

''Cassandra, you're in the real world now. The life you have I pay for—your car, your apartment, your clothes, even your food. You've never earned your way, and I don't think you can now. Marry Somner; it's in everybody's best interest.''

Cassandra stood. Her large eyes swept back and forth across her father's face; her breathing was forced from anger and hurt. ''Best interests? Am I another one of your business deals? A piece of property to trade? What can you gain from selling me to Somner? You're richer than he or his father. Your company is bigger. What?'' she screamed, feeling like nothing more than a piece of merchandise that has already been sold and discarded.

Gregory Leeds stood and walked from behind his desk. He had hoped Cassandra would have accepted his advice without theatrics. Yet in the back of his mind, he was aware of a new spark in her eyes, a spark that combined anger, resentment, and something else. . . . *Challenge, perhaps*, he thought.

He went to his daughter, but as he reached out to embrace her she stepped back.

''No! I'm not a little child anymore.''

Gregory sighed. ''I wish that were true.''

''Father, please don't force me to do this,'' she pleaded in a low voice.

''I'm sorry, Cassie,'' he said, using the name he had not used since she was a child. ''But you've no choice. You really can do nothing else. Being a good wife—a good mother—is just as important as what I do.''

''Damn it! I can do something with my life. I'm not ready to be married off. Please, Father, let me show you that I can do something.''

Gregory took a deep breath and gazed intently at Cassandra. As she had pleaded with him her eyes had grown stronger, her gaze both conciliatory and challenging at the same time. Yet Gregory knew that she was just trying to avoid responsibility.

"What can you do?"

Cassandra saw a look of challenge, mixed with a look of hopelessness, on her father's face. He didn't believe her. *You're wrong, Father,* she said silently. Straightening her shoulders, she stared directly into his eyes.

"I can do anything! Anything! Give me one of your companies to run and I'll prove it to you."

"Just like that? Just give you a company to run? Don't be ridiculous." But in the back of his mind, he felt the germ of an emerging idea. "Anything, Cassandra?"

"That's what I said."

Nodding his head, Gregory returned to his desk. "All right."

Cassandra's breath exploded. She had hoped against hope that her father would listen to her and let her try to find a path for her life. Although she hadn't known what to expect from today's meeting, victory had been only a small glimmer in her mind. Now she was soaring, and she smiled radiantly at her father.

"What?" she asked eagerly. "Which company?" Visions of boardrooms filled with powerful executives all listening obsequiously to her every word filled her mind . . . lunches at which she commanded all the attention, making deals at the drop of a hat . . . "Tell me, Father, please."

Gregory gazed at his daughter's radiant face and held his words back for a moment. She was flushed with victory; it was a look he wanted to remember for a long time. "Tomorrow. I have to think about it tonight."

"Okay," she said quickly. Then she paused as another thought struck her. "You aren't planning to just make me a figurehead, an adornment, are you? I really do want to show you that I can stand on my own two feet."

"You have my word that whatever company I give you will be yours to run, or ruin," he promised solemnly. "Now, I have work to do. Be here at nine tomorrow morning."

"Very well, Father," she said. Then she went around his desk and kissed him on the cheek. "Thank you," she whispered. A moment later she was at the door.

"Cassandra," her father called. With her hand wavering on the doorknob, she turned back to look at him. "There is one more thing. I closed your apartment down two months ago and bought out the lease. All your things are at the house."

Cassandra's smile froze on her lips. "Why?"

"When you failed to call after a month, I decided that I was through supporting you. If you had used your credit cards any time in the past two months, you would have learned that. If I hadn't sent you the ticket home, you would not have been able to leave Greece. Cassandra, you are welcome to stay at home until you either marry Somner, or you take my job offer."

Cassandra knew her father was very, very serious. She also knew that she had been given one more chance and was not about to lose it. Forcing herself not to think about her loss of freedom, Cassandra left the office.

Kirk North hung up the phone, sat back, and closed his eyes. Although it was only four o'clock, it had been a long day in a series of long days. Kirk had been the general manager of the Twin Rivers Ranch for three-and-a-half years of his seven-year employment and had never had as bad a year as this one.

It had been a lean, dry year. Beef prices were down, and the herd of Appaloosa he had been breeding so carefully had been hit with disease. He had managed to save a fair number of them but would be unable to sell the horses as planned.

The fiscal year was ending in a week, and the ranch would show a loss for the second year in a row. He had just gotten off the phone with Murray Charter, the comptroller of the corporation that owned the ranch. He had been honest about the year and been surprised to hear no chastisement in the man's voice.

"You'll just have to do better next year," Charter had told him.

Something about that bothered Kirk. It was almost as if the man didn't care. But Kirk did. Ranching, and being a success, were important to him. Why wasn't it important to the Leeds Corporation?

This wasn't the first time that question had crossed his mind. He had felt the same way last year after the year-end audit. He had received a raise, which had taken him by surprise—so much so that he'd contacted Charter and refused the raise.

The comptroller had argued with him, but Kirk had been adamant. "When I do the job properly. When I show a profit, then I'll take the raise," he'd told the man. His words and tone had brooked no argument.

What would happen now? he wondered.

Shaking his head, he stood and stretched his six-foot two-inch frame. Easing his stiff muscles, Kirk wished he were on a horse, instead of sitting in a chair today. Then he ran his fingers through his wavy brown hair. As he did, his eyes fell on the aerial photograph of the ranch.

Kirk enjoyed his responsibility of the one-hundred-and-twenty-thousand acres of prime Arizona land, along with the thirty-thousand head of cattle, and five-hundred head of Appaloosa horse stock. The ranch house itself was large—eight bedrooms, five baths, a formal living room, and a dining room that could seat thirty. There was a library, a study, and a den. There was also an immense kitchen and servants' quarters.

At one time, before the large corporations had invaded the area of ranching, Twin Rivers had been the center of ranching in the Phoenix area. But now, like many other of the old-time spreads, it was a corporate venture.

The large house was no longer used as a place to live, except occasionally when the corporate people came and used the two main suites upstairs. The main floor of the house was the ranch's offices; Kirk's office had once been the library.

A hundred yards from the main house was his own house. As the general manager, he was entitled to private quarters. Near his own house was another house, smaller than his, but just as nice. Right now it was being used to house the only female ranch hand working at Twin Rivers. Set back another thirty yards from his house was the main housing complex, where the unmarried ranch hands bunked.

Kirk's eyes wandered along the aerial map, taking in the various ranges. On the far side of the ranch was a five-thousand acre farm, where they grew a good deal of the grain and hay.

A series of livestock corrals were set a quarter-mile from

the main house, along with a complex of barns, stables, and silos.

Why wasn't the Leeds Corporation worried about taking a loss two years in a row? he asked himself again. The puzzle was beginning to show signs of becoming an obsession with him. Something wasn't right, and he wanted to know what that something was.

Returning to his desk, he sat and faced the computer. A moment later, he was gazing at long rows of figures. Even as he did, he laughed and his face softened.

Kirk wondered just how a rancher from fifty or a hundred years ago would react to modern ranching, run by corporations and computers and boardroom logic.

"Not very well," he told himself aloud. Kirk knew that there was one important aspect of ranching that big business did not understand, and probably would never understand. Ranching was a business, but it was also a very personal thing. You could not be a rancher if you felt nothing for the land around you. That's where the corporations made their mistakes.

But then, Kirk could not imagine himself doing anything but ranching. Especially after what he had been through before. Shaking away those thoughts, Kirk concentrated on the ranch's figures, and on the thought that continued to plague his conscience. Kirk knew that he would do his best to find out what was going on, no matter how long it took.

Cassandra lay restlessly in her bed, listening to the chiming of an old grandfather clock. Her mind was churning endlessly, and she could not make herself relax at all. She had still not fully recovered from this afternoon's harsh confrontation with her father and had hoped that she would be able to talk to him tonight, but that hope had been dismissed when she'd spoken to her mother, who had been on her way out of the house when she'd come in.

"Cassie," Eleanor Leeds had cried happily when she'd seen her daughter.

Cassie had hugged her mother through the ermine stole and kissed her cheek. Then she'd seen her mother's brow wrinkle with a frown as she'd studied her.

"I take it you've already talked with your father?"

"Yes," Cassandra had said in a sad voice.

"He loves you very much, dear; he wants you to have a good life," Eleanor had begun but was interrupted by the chauffeur.

"It's five o'clock, Mrs. Leeds."

"So it is," Eleanor had said with a nod. "We'll talk tomorrow, dear. I have a benefit that will last very late."

"Is Father going?" she'd asked.

"For a little while. But, he has some people in from Europe. You know how he is . . ."

When her mother had fairly flown out of the house in a whoosh of silk, Cassandra had gone to her bedroom, undressed, and taken a shower. After that, she'd eaten, gone to the library, and chosen a book at random. By ten o'clock, she could not keep her eyes open and realized she'd been up almost twenty-four hours. But as soon as she lay down, her mind began to speed up.

Realizing that what was bothering her was the uncertainty of her future, Cassandra's low laughter echoed in the silent bedroom. It was the same uncertainty that had been a constant part of her for the past year.

No more, she told herself, knowing that tomorrow would

bring the change she was hoping for. Tomorrow would be the beginning of her future, and she was ready.

With that thought, Cassandra finally fell into a deep dreamless sleep.

Gregory Leeds sat behind his desk, absently going over the day's accumulation of memos. It was two o'clock in the morning, and after leaving his European associates at the Pierre, he had returned to his office to solve yet another problem—Cassandra.

He had spent several hours looking over his companies, trying to decide which one to place her in. He could not afford to have her hurt any important deals, yet he wanted her to see what the business world was like.

He believed that after a month or two, Cassandra would call him and concede. Then she would marry Somner Barwell, as he had planned for her to do. The marriage would benefit him because it would mean that Jonathan Barwell, Somner's father, and he would become business associates rather than competitors. Presently, the two corporations were in a fearsome battle.

Gregory knew that he, Barwell, and several others of their level were like the old royalty. And when royalty married, it was a merging of power and wealth for their mutual benefit. Although the names and titles had changed over the centuries, the basic concepts were the same.

Gregory glanced at a memo from Murray Charter about Twin Rivers. Something clicked in his mind, and he picked it up. It was short and simple.

Twelve-percent loss over last year. North's figures tentative but seem to match our own projections. Should we try to give him a raise this year?

As soon as Gregory read the last line, he remembered what had happened. Kirk North was the G.M. of the ranch, and had been so when they'd bought the property three years ago. He had shown himself to be a sharp man, with good managing abilities and a quick mind. He was a college graduate and a good worker. When he'd turned down the raise last year, Gregory had been surprised and asked Murray about it.

"He takes his job seriously. He said he hadn't made a profit, so he didn't earn the raise."

"Give it to him anyway," Gregory had ordered. It was not North's fault that the ranch did not show a profit. The Leeds Corporation had bought the ranch for two reasons. And for neither of those reasons were there supposed to be any profits—yet.

A month after he and Murray had discussed Kirk North, Murray had reported that North had again requested his raise to be withdrawn and had sent a check to the comptroller for the exact amount of the raise.

"It's his choice," Gregory had finally told Murray, but his respect for the G.M. had increased, and the memory of the incident had never really been forgotten.

Then a smile formed on Gregory Leeds' face. He knew exactly which company to turn over to his daughter . . . if she would take it in the first place.

No, he would give her no choice in this, he decided. He hoped that by using the ranch, and her worst fears, he would force her to give up immediately. If that didn't work, the assured guarantee of not showing a profit in the next year would solve the problem.

However, according to his plan, in two more years the ranch would show a profit. Everything had been very carefully calculated down to the last possible penny. But, only three men in the world knew how those profits would be attained, and those two others would not be telling anyone else, for the utmost secrecy had to be maintained in order to successfully accomplish his plan.

Yes, it was Twin Rivers for Cassie.

"The Twin Rivers Corporation?" Cassandra echoed. She was seated next to her father on his long leather couch. She had been there for half an hour, sipping coffee and waiting for her father to tell her what company he was going to let her take over.

He had repeatedly asked her if she was sure of her decision, asking her three different times if she wouldn't rather marry Somner Barwell and continue to enjoy her leisurely life of freedom.

Each time he had asked she'd given him an adamant and simple no. Then he told her the name of the company.

"Where exactly is this company?" she asked as she racked her memory, trying to recall even a single mention of its name. Sadly she realized her father had never spoken of it.

"In Arizona, just outside of Phoenix," Gregory Leeds told her as he studied her face carefully.

Cassandra laughed lightly and shook her head. She had never been to Phoenix, or to Arizona at all, for that matter, nor had she ever had the desire to. "I didn't know Leeds International was involved with old-age homes," she jested. "Or cactus."

"We're not," he said but did not elaborate.

"Pray tell, Father, what is Twin Rivers Corporation?"

"A ranch," he said simply.

"A ranch?" Cassandra echoed with a smile. "With cows?"

"With cattle and barns and corrals and . . . horses."

Cassandra couldn't stop her jaw from dropping. The blood drained from her face, and she fought desperately for breath.

Gregory Leeds watched his daughter turn the color of newly fallen snow, and saw, too, the sharp rising and falling of her chest as she fought to digest his words, but he held his own emotions in check; too much was at stake.

The world swam before her eyes. She felt as though she were falling, arcing through the air and landing on her head and right side. She could hear the snapping of her bones and feel the lancing pain. But then she reached deep inside herself for strength and forced herself to breathe normally. A moment later her vision cleared, and she stared at her father with reproach and unvoiced accusation.

"Do you want to call it off?" Gregory asked in a gentle voice.

Yes!!! her mind screamed silently. But from that same place where she had found the strength to fight away her fear, she found the strength to stand up to him. "I'd rather die first," Cassandra told him in an icy voice.

Gregory kept his face emotionless. His heart was pounding as it had not done in years. And despite his desire to have her turn down his offer, he was strangely glad she had not done so.

"All right, Cassandra," he said a moment later. Then he reached for a thick manila envelope that was lying on the coffee table. "This is the information that you'll have to study before you go to Arizona. You have a week to prepare yourself. Elizabeth will show you to an office that you can use."

Cassandra realized from the tone of his voice that their

meeting was over. Standing, she stared at him. "Thank you, Father," she said as she took the envelope. Walking quickly from his office, she prayed that he had not seen the way her hand had been trembling when she'd taken the packet.

Outside, with the door closed, she leaned against its hardness. She took several deep breaths, and then started toward her father's secretary. *What have I done?* she asked herself.

The sun's bright rays bathed the rolling meadow in golden light. The velvet swath of grass, which spread out for a hundred unspoiled acres, was broken in strategic spots by randomly placed hedges of varying heights.

Cassandra loved the way the warm breeze caressed her face beneath the riding hat and let the way she felt show in the smile she favored the others with. Her long hair, tied back in a traditional ponytail, escaped from beneath the hat and reached almost to the saddle.

Today was a special day for Cassandra. Today she was riding Magik, her father's Arabian steeplechase mount. He had promised her a year before that if she took first prize in her riding and jumping class, she could ride Magik.

Cassandra had worked hard to win. Now she was being rewarded for her work.

"Remember, no jumping," her father cautioned again as he rode next to her.

Cassandra nodded, intent on the job of controlling the large Thoroughbred and equally proud of her ability to do so. She and her father posted in unison, and Cassandra felt the excitement build within her, enhanced by the power of the magnificent horse she rode.

"Can we go faster?" she asked.

"Carefully," her father said, increasing their pace to a slow gallop.

Cassandra held the reins carefully and, for just an instant, she felt Magik try to go faster, but she held him back.

"Very good," her father said. "Always remember that you must maintain control. And that, Cassandra, is true for business also."

But Cassandra didn't hear him. She was giving her full attention to the horse. She had controlled him, and with that knowledge had come a feeling of power. There was very little Cassandra had ever been afraid of, and now, in the instant she had learned that she could control the large horse, she feared even less.

"Faster!" she cried to her father, setting herself in the saddle and moving with the horse. The breeze on her face grew stronger, and the hedges she rode past became a blur.

"Cassandra!" her father shouted.

Cassandra turned to smile at him. He was already twenty feet behind her, and she saw a frown of concern on his face. "Slow down!" he ordered, his voice loud and commanding.

Cassandra didn't. She knew she could control the horse and wanted to ride forever. Before she could turn forward again, she saw the panic on her father's face and heard him shout again.

"The hedges! Cassandra, the hedges!"

Cassandra turned just as Magik reached the highest hedge jump on the course. Before she could prepare herself, the horse, who had been trained to jump whatever was in front of him, launched himself.

She screamed even as she tried to set herself properly in

the saddle. Because she was unprepared, her movements threw the horse off stride. Magik's front legs did not fully clear the top of the hedge.

Everything moved in slow motion. Cassandra screamed as she held onto the reins. The horse rose in the air, and Cassandra felt it hit the hedge. Then the world was spinning upside down. The next thing she saw was the green grass coming up to meet her. Pain exploded in her head, and spread to every part of her body.

The horse had cleared the jump, but not with enough room to land properly. Its legs crumpled beneath it, and it rolled sideways, catching Cassandra beneath it. Panicked, the horse fought to stand and did. Then it began to run madly, trying to dislodge the limp, almost lifeless form that was caught in one stirrup—the form that was a nine-year-old girl named Cassandra Leeds, who throughout the quarter-mile the horse dragged her, felt and saw everything in a whirlwind of pain and kaleidoscopic madness. When her father caught and stopped the horse and then bent over her, she saw the fear covering his face. Only then, when she felt his hand on her cheek, did darkness end the pain.

"No!" Cassandra screamed, sitting up and wrapping her arms around her shaking body. "Please don't let it start again," she cried.

Standing, Cassandra pulled on a thick terry bathrobe and turned the bedtable lamp on. "Please," she whispered, "don't let the nightmares start again."

Cassandra took a deep breath and walked across the room to look at the miniature grandfather clock.

Midnight had come and gone and with it, Cassandra knew, had gone her ability to sleep.

Cassandra took several more deep calming breaths before

sitting on the bentwood rocker, the very same chair her mother had nursed her in when she was a baby. Looking around the room, Cassandra tried to capture the old feelings of her childhood. But as she glanced around the room she had grown up in, those feelings remained hidden.

She had always known that she was one of the more fortunate people. She had never wanted for anything, and that should have made her happy. But it hadn't, she realized as she tried not to let the tears of sadness and pain break free.

I never wanted those things that everyone bought me. I wanted something that I couldn't have, she told herself, remembering all the lonely times when she'd gone to her father, hoping to see love and warmth in his eyes, not presents filling his hands.

Her memory was good; it had always been so. She could remember all the way back to her fourth birthday. She remembered the happiness of her childhood, when everything was simple, and she knew, without any doubts, that she was loved and wanted.

As she'd grown older, the security of her emotions had fled, and she'd learned how to put a shell around her to make people believe that she was still the same happy girl, although it was a lie.

Has my life been a lie? she asked herself, feeling the tears reach the rim of her eyes and wash over onto her cheeks. *Who am I?*

Up to the age of nine, Cassandra could have answered that question easily. "I am Cassandra Leeds. My daddy is Gregory Leeds."

She remembered a reporter interviewing her father when she was eight. It was at home, and she was sitting in a small chair off to one side. The man had turned to her, a smile on his face. "What are you going to be when you grow up?" he'd asked.

"The president of Leeds International, like Daddy," she'd replied instantly, smiling at her father and bathing within his wide and proud smile.

But that had been at eight. At nine and a half, her father didn't smile like that anymore. Neither did Cassie. Instead Cassandra had nightmares every night. They had started in the hospital and continued until she'd turned nineteen. For ten long years, Cassandra Leeds had been haunted and terrified by her dreams. The dream was always the same dream, and it always ended the same way. She would wake up screaming, her body bathed in sweat, her cries constant and heartrending.

And tonight her nightmare had returned.

Unable to stop the memories, Cassandra thought back to the accident. She had lost control of the horse, and it had been her own fault that she'd almost died.

But she hadn't died. She had been in a coma for three weeks after the accident, which had left her with a broken pelvis, a broken leg, a fractured ankle, a concussion, and a herniated disk in her neck.

When she had woken in the hospital, she did so screaming, until her mother had calmed her down with soothing words and gentle strokes.

The pain was almost unbearable, but she'd survived. It took three months before she could walk without crutches and another month before she was free of most of the pain. But she'd learned one thing: She would never be free of her memories of that day.

A half-year later, her father had taken her back to Long

Island. He hadn't said why they were going, he had just told her they were going, in the same unsmiling way he'd spoken to her ever since the accident.

When they reached the riding club, Cassandra began to cry. "What's wrong?" her father asked.

"I don't want to be here."

"You have to be here, Cassie; it's important."

"Why?" she'd asked, trying to hold back the tears.

"You were hurt very badly, and if you don't get on a horse again, you may never ride again. You're going to ride today," he told her.

"M-M-M-Magik?"

"Not Magik. Cassie, I promise you that Magik will never hurt you again. I had him destroyed."

Cassandra had stared at him, her eyes wide with horror. "You . . ." But Cassandra hadn't been able to say anything more. Her voice had become frozen. She'd just stared at him. Then she'd smelled the horses. The scent was over-powering; she began to shake.

At the stable, Gregory Leeds had made Cassandra follow him and stand next to him as they saddled two horses. Cassandra's shaking wouldn't stop.

When the horses were ready, her father had bent to lift her into the saddle. It was then that Cassandra had screamed over and over again and started to run away.

"Come back here!" Gregory Leeds had shouted.

Cassandra had kept on running.

And I've been running ever since, she told herself. *I've been running away from fear and from life.*

"No more," she whispered. Cassandra knew that she couldn't run away anymore. She wanted to be able to live her own life and be happy again. The last time she had been happy was when she was nine. Eighteen years was too long.

And Cassandra saw that for the past eighteen years she had done everything in her power to hide from reality. She had roamed the world as a spoiled child, who had grown into a spoiled woman. She had never once tried to do something worthwhile. In Greece, she had come to a small understanding of why she had been doing some of those things. She had wanted to make her father angry enough to show her he cared.

But he hadn't. All he wanted from her was another corporate merger. Cassandra drew in a shuddering breath. Her father was trying to bend her to his will; and he was using the one thing she feared most in life to accomplish his own desires. Standing, Cassandra fanned the embers of anger within her mind. *Not this time, Father,* she promised.

In that harsh moment of deep self examination, Cassandra began to repair the walls of her defenses so that no one would ever know how vulnerable she was. Cassandra made up her mind to take on the job her father had offered.

No one, she vowed, would see her fear. No one would get past the protective walls she'd erected around herself.

Chapter Three

Stretching long legs before him, Kirk North relieved the dull cramps of the five-hour flight. He was thankful that the Leeds Corporation did not stint on expenses for their employees and that he was flying first-class rather than being packed like a sardine in coach.

Far below the 747's window, Kirk saw the lush green hills of the Northeast. He also knew, by the time of the flight as well as his own knowledge of the country, that they were over New Jersey.

"Last call, Mr. North; we'll be landing in a half-hour. Can I get you another cup of coffee, or anything at all?" asked a doe-eyed stewardess who smiled with an open invitation.

Kirk shook his head. "Thank you, anyway."

The woman seemed disappointed but took it in stride as she went to the seat behind him and asked the woman seated there if she wanted another drink. Even as she spoke, her voice was filtered from Kirk's consciousness while his own troubled thoughts took over again.

Two days before, he'd received a call from the comptroller of Leeds, requesting his presence in New York. The boss wanted to see him, and he was certain of the reason. The books had been closed four days before on Twin Rivers' fiscal year, and it had not been a good one.

For the second year in a row, the ranch had shown a loss, not a profit. Although Kirk had done everything in his power to make the ranch reach into the black this year, he had been defeated by the low market price of beef, the high cost of supplemental feeding, and a harsh rampaging disease that had struck the Appaloosa herd, cutting down the number of head available to be sold, and therefore ending the chance to make money on the horses this year. But the worst loss had been the death of the primary Appaloosa stallion who had sired so many of Twin Rivers' foals. The disease had killed him, and had set back the horse-breeding operation until a new but proven stud could be brought to the ranch.

Of course, none of those reasons mattered. It was his responsibility to make Twin Rivers profitable, just as it was his responsibility to accept the blame if it failed.

Kirk looked at his watch. It was nine o'clock. He planned on registering at the hotel before a general meeting at eleven thirty, then he would have lunch with Murray Charter, after which he would have his meeting with Gregory Leeds at two thirty.

Kirk fully expected to be fired and was prepared for just that. The only question that nagged at his thoughts was why they had asked him to come to New York instead of terminating him by official letter.

I'll find out soon enough, he told himself. Then he chased

away his troubled thoughts, rested his head on the seatback,
and thought about the new stud he would be signing the
papers for in Wyoming—the horse he hoped would be able
to replenish the Twin Rivers' stock for many years to come,
if, he realized, he was still general manager when he left
New York.

"I'm sorry, Somner, but I have an important appointment at three thirty. Perhaps another day," Cassandra said
with the hope of stalling Somner until she was gone so that
she would not have to continue explaining her actions to
him.

"Please, Cassie, we need to speak. I've already made a
reservation at Le Blanc for twelve thirty," Somner Barwell
stated.

"I'm really pushed for time—"

"I've been patient for over three months, Cassie. I
haven't pressed you; I haven't chased after you. The least
you could do is see me and tell me what's going on."

Cassandra knew he was right. She could not just up and
leave again without telling him the real reason. *Why didn't
you chase me? Why didn't you put up a fight? Why did you
accept what I did so easily?* she asked him silently. But she
knew him well enough to answer the question herself.
Somner Barwell had no need to chase or fight for her; he
expected her to be his.

"All right, Somner, I'll be there at twelve thirty." With
that, she hung up the phone gently and looked at her watch.
It was eleven.

She knew that she had been wrong in avoiding Somner
Barwell's phone calls, and this morning before she'd left
home, he'd called again. She had pleaded an appointment,
without saying what it was but had promised to call him

later in the morning. Now that she had, she felt a little better.

Sighing, Cassandra banished the thoughts of Somner and, as she had been doing every day for the last week, turned back to the papers that covered her desk. She had become so immersed in learning how to use the computer and then reviewing the figures and reports of her new corporation, that the week, including the weekend, had flown by as quickly as a jet plane. She had learned much about the ranch but understood there was still a lot more to take in.

The Twin Rivers Ranch was a fairly large operation, employing over seventy people. The ranch itself was being managed by a man named Kirk North—a cowboy, Cassandra thought tersely. According to everything she'd studied, North had been doing a good job, just not good enough to make a profit. She hoped she would be able to change that.

"I have to change that!" she stated aloud to the silent office. "I have to," she whispered.

The fiscal year of the Twin Rivers Corporation had ended four days before, and the rough audit figures on her desk had been sent over that very morning by Murray Charter, the comptroller of Leeds International. She had been going over the figures all morning, comparing them to the audit statements of the last four years, in an effort to find a weak spot that she could pinpoint as the object of her first change.

Forty-five minutes later she glanced at her watch and realized that she had to get going or she'd be late for lunch. Sighing, Cassandra stood and straightened her clothing. She felt a slight edge of nervousness and knew that today's lunch would not be easy, but it was something that had to be done.

Cassandra decided that she owed Somner the truth. She must tell him why she could not marry him.

I can do it, she told herself firmly as she started to the ladies' room to freshen up for her confrontation with Somner.

"What I don't understand, Mr. Charter, is why the Leeds Corporation is so complacent about the loss," Kirk ventured after Murray Charter finished his statements.

Nothing was making sense to Kirk. From the moment he'd entered Charter's office, he'd been treated as a visiting executive, not a man about to be fired. Within twenty minutes of sitting down, the comptroller had complimented him on his performance as the G.M. three separate times.

"Because we had projected this loss when we took over the ranch two years ago. Everything is going according to our projections," replied the slim well-dressed comptroller in an even voice.

Kirk, no stranger to business projections and machinations, could not accept that glossy answer. "Even the horses?"

"Not exactly, but yes. You see, Kirk, when we set up our projections, we took into account a number of things that might happen. Although we did not specifically earmark a problem with the horse stock, it isn't major enough to worry about. In two years, the horse sales will be back on target."

Kirk studied the smooth-talking man for several silent seconds before responding. When he did, it was quick and dry. "Then why am I here, if I'm not being fired?"

Murray Charter laughed, but Kirk saw that the smile didn't reach the man's eyes. A strange chill of warning settled in the nape of his neck as he waited for the man to speak.

"That's something else. Kirk, before I get into that, I want to reiterate that we at Leeds feel you are doing an excellent job."

"But?"

"No buts; that's a fact," the comptroller stated. Yet with his next words, Kirk heard a subtle change in Charter's voice. "However, when you return to Arizona, you will be bringing someone with you. Our new vice president of the Twin Rivers Corporation."

Kirk held himself in check for a moment, refusing to let the effect of the announcement show on his face. He realized that he'd been very fortunate in the last two years in not having a corporation man breathing down his neck. But his luck had just run out. When he was sure of himself, he nodded his head slowly. "I can live with that," he said stoically. "Who will it be?"

Murray Charter said nothing for a moment, and Kirk could not read his expression. "Mr. Leeds wants to personally fill you in on those details," the comptroller stated. "And now," he added as he looked at his watch, "I think we should grab some lunch."

Before either Charter or Kirk could stand, the comptroller's intercom buzzed. Kirk tried to relax as the man picked up the phone.

"All right. Ten minutes!" Charter said. When he hung up the phone, he looked at Kirk with apology written across his features. "Kirk, I'm afraid I'll have to cancel. There seems to be an emergency at our German subsidiary. I'll be tied up for quite a while."

"No problem," Kirk said as he stood and extended his hand.

Charter shook his hand firmly. "But I did remember that Le Blanc was a favorite of yours. There's a table reserved for you for twelve fifteen."

"Thank you, Mr. Charter. I'll see you later," Kirk said as he withdrew his hand and started to leave the office, not the least upset at losing his lunchmate. Right now he wanted to be alone to think about what Charter had told him.

After leaving the comptroller's office and taking the elevator to the lobby, Kirk then walked the three blocks to the restaurant. Le Blanc was indeed Kirk's favorite restaurant in New York. Whenever he was here, he made it a point to dine there.

Entering the comfortably lit restaurant, Kirk saw that lunch was in full swing. He gave the maître d' his name and a moment later was being escorted to his table.

"Monsieur Charter will be joining you shortly?" the man asked.

"He won't be able to make it," Kirk replied.

"Ah . . . a shame; he misses a wonderful meal. *Bon appétit,* Monsieur North," the maître d' said with a practiced gesture while at the same time presenting Kirk with the menu.

A moment later a white-jacketed waiter appeared with a serving tray. "Would you prefer white or red?" he asked.

"White," Kirk replied and then watched the man pour the wine into the glass. When the waiter was gone, Kirk took a sip of the dry wine and opened the menu.

After perusing it carefully, Kirk settled on stuffed Dover sole. As soon as he put the menu down, the waiter reappeared and took his order.

With that done, Kirk let his thoughts roam. He tried to work out the strange puzzle that the Leeds Corporation kept putting in front of him; he sensed that something wasn't right, but just what that was, he had been unable to discern.

Although he didn't relish the idea of having a company man looking over his shoulder, Kirk could not complain. It was not a good time for people in ranching, and he still had his job, a job he loved.

His train of thought was suddenly interrupted as his eyes were drawn to a tall woman walking past his table. He knew he was staring at her but could not stop himself.

She had long, almost jet black hair that fell to the middle of her back, complementing the ivory business suit she wore. She was tall, at least five-eight. Kirk appreciated her height and the way she did not try to hide it. The business suit fit her as if it had been tailored just for her body, revealing a full, ripe figure even as it contained it in conservative lines.

The even sway of her hips was accented by the linen material of the skirt and the gentle movement of her hair. But it wasn't until she reached her table, just down the aisle from his, that Kirk's breath seemed to catch in his throat. Because it was only then that he saw her face.

Her eyes were large, wide-set, and absolutely magnificent. Even at a distance of ten feet, he could see sparks of emerald green blazing from within their hazel depths. Her face, too, was an almost classic type of beauty: Her cheekbones were perfectly formed but not overly prominent; her chin was rounded without a dimple or mark. Her nose was straight and aquiline, and her mouth was like the double set of a hunting bow. Her neck was long and slender and disappeared within the beige collar of her blouse. At the base of her throat was a single gold chain.

Although he'd never seen her before, Kirk knew with his

one long glance, that the woman who was sitting down not far from him, was a very special person.

And the man she's with is a very lucky man, he said to himself.

Breaking the magnetic attraction of the woman, Kirk made himself think about his meeting with Murray Charter and of the vagaries of fate. After all, he reasoned, he should not be enjoying a costly lunch at the expense of the company that employed him; rather, he should have been wondering about where he would find his next job.

A moment later the waiter brought his food and, with the requisite flourishes, served Kirk elegantly.

Cassandra entered Le Blanc with her usual air of confidence, smiling and nodding her head to those who acknowledged her arrival even as she looked around for Somner. Spotting him, she strode directly to his table, uncaring of the many eyes that marked her progress. She had learned long ago that males of all ages, whether alone or with a companion, watched any good-looking woman.

None of that bothered Cassandra while she walked to Somner's table, but when she turned around by her chair, she found herself the focus of a handsome man sitting two tables away—a man who had the most intriguing eyes she'd ever seen.

Forcefully she broke the unexpectedly powerful gaze and smiled at Somner. "And not a minute late."

"For which I will be eternally grateful," Somner said with his own dashing smile.

He stood and started around the table, but Cassandra held up her hand and seated herself. A half-minute later the waiter appeared to pour their wine.

"I've already ordered," Somner said. "You did say our time was limited."

"Of course."

"Veal Francese. I know how much you like it."

"Thank you," Cassandra said, trying to keep the irritation out of her voice. Somner always ordered for them—always.

"Cassie," Somner began, but Cassandra lifted her glass and held it aloft.

"A toast."

"In honor of?" he asked.

"My new job."

Somner's smile flattened. "Job? Why?"

"Because I needed it."

"You needed a job . . . What about me?"

Cassandra couldn't help the smile caused by his startled reaction. "You don't need a job; you have one."

"That's not what I mean. I need you also."

"Me, or what I represent?" Cassandra asked. There was no malice in her tone, and the question was asked honestly.

"What's that supposed to mean?" Somner asked in a coarse voice, his lips thinning until they became little more than a narrow line.

With the perfect timing of the insensitive, the waiter appeared with their lunch. They stayed silent while the waiter, with delicate maneuvers, placed the plates before Cassandra and Somner, after which he held a long wooden pepper mill aloft and looked at Cassandra.

"No, thank you," she said pleasantly. Somner waved him brusquely away.

Cassandra refused to look at Somner for a moment as she picked up her silverware and cut a small piece of veal. She had told herself before entering the restaurant that she would be open and honest with him. She did not want to be catty, but she had to make him understand what she needed for herself.

"Are you ready to answer me?" Somner asked.

"Can't we enjoy our lunch first?"

"Which means that if we talk now, we won't be able to eat?"

"That depends on you. The veal is delicious. Thank you for choosing it," Cassandra added as she put another small piece into her mouth.

"Cassandra, I've waited three months for this . . ."

Cassandra put down her silverware and took a deep breath. "You're right, Somner. I don't mean to procrastinate. You have every right to an explanation, and an apology."

"All I want is you."

"What good would I be if I don't want to be married now? Somner, I'm sorry for not speaking out sooner. I just feel that I need some time to learn about myself, to work and see what I'm capable of before getting married."

"Marriage has nothing to do with work."

"I think it does."

"Then all you had to do was ask. I can give you a job in one of my companies, and we can get married also."

Cassandra ignored his last few words. "Really? What kind of a job?"

"You have a natural flair for promotion. You'd make a great P.R. lady," Somner stated with a proud smile.

Irritated, she was hard-pressed to hold back her anger. "Because of my social contacts? Or would I be good at P.R. because you don't think I have any talent for real business?"

"Don't put words in my mouth," Somner snapped loudly.

"No, that's your game."

"Cassie, why are we arguing?" he asked in a more controlled voice. "I love you. I want to marry you."

"And I want to live the life I choose. I want to do for myself before I have someone else taking care of me. Is that so hard to understand?"

"Yes!" Somner Barwell, always the calm aristocrat, shouted the word. Several people turned to look at them but quickly averted their eyes.

Cassandra tried to keep her anger in check but found it harder with every passing heated moment.

Once again Cassandra reinforced her earlier intentions. "Somner, I know that we've been together for the last year and that we had a wonderful time. But nothing stands still; people change—I've changed. I need some direction in my life before I settle down. That's what I'm trying to find now."

"Some direction or some other man?" he challenged.

"I won't dignify that with an answer," Cassandra whispered icily.

"Where have you been for the last three months? Who were you with?" The harshness in Somner's voice was amplified within the confines of the restaurant, and once again several heads turned to look at them.

"Don't let your fragile ego get in the way of this conversation!" she snapped. Then she forced herself to speak in a calmer tone. "I was in Greece, trying to understand why I wasn't with you," she replied truthfully.

"I find that hard to believe."

"That's your problem!" Cassandra was very conscious of the people who were now openly staring at them, and strangely, of the man she'd seen just before sitting down. But he apparently had better manners than the others. He was not looking at them; he was signing his check.

"Cassie, I want us to marry."

"Why?"

"Because we love each other."

"I don't think so, Somner," Cassandra whispered. But the look in his eyes told her he would not accept her answer.

"I do!" he stated, accenting his words with a sharp slap of his hand on the table.

Cassandra stared at him.

"Cassie, we're good for each other. Everyone says so. Even our parents think our marriage would be a wonderful match."

"A wonderful match? Does that mean love, convenience, or just the easiest way to consolidate our fathers' business dealings?" Before Somner could respond, Cassandra held up her hand to ward off his next words.

"What about me? Do what I think and feel make any difference? Do I get a say in this, or has the decision been made by you and our parents?" Without realizing it, Cassandra's voice had risen loudly, but she no longer cared.

"That's what we're here for."

Cassandra's hard-fought control failed, and her angry voice was directed loudly at Somner Barwell's inflexible attitude and lack of understanding.

"No! That's what *I* came here for. *You* came here to tell me what *you* want, and what *everyone* else wants. Well, I'll tell you something, Somner Barwell. I don't give a hoot what anyone else thinks I should be doing. I'll do what I damn well please, and I'll live my life for myself, not for the people around me!"

Standing, Cassandra pushed her chair back, drew her

shoulders straight, and marched out of the restaurant. She ignored the startled stares, the knowing snickers hidden behind the backs of hands, and with every ounce of dignity, emerged onto Madison Avenue into the brilliant afternoon sun.

How dare he treat me like that! I tried. I tried to tell him how I felt, but all he did was tell me what he wanted. Tears of anger stung her eyes, but she blinked them away as she walked quickly toward the Leeds Building and the sanctuary of her office. When she turned onto Fifth Avenue, she heard Somner call her name. Cassandra didn't stop but increased her speed.

After the endlessly long two-block walk, she reached the building and, stepping quickly inside, headed toward the elevators. Behind her, Somner shouted her name again. At the far elevator bank, she pressed the call button several angry times. *Leave me alone!* she wanted to yell. But Somner's footsteps grew louder.

"Cassie, listen to me," Somner said when he reached her.

Cassandra refused to turn. Her back was stiff as she concentrated on the elevator door. "We have nothing else to say."

"We have a lot to say! Cassandra, I'm sorry. I don't want to lose you. If you want to work, I'll buy you a company. Just name it!"

Cassandra took a deep breath and, turning to face him, chased her anger away. "You just can't see it, can you, Somner?"

"Whatever you want, I'll buy it for you. You want to be a businesswoman? I'll buy a business for you," he told her. "Just marry me."

Cassandra suddenly understood. Somner Barwell was a

product of his parents and their generation. He had been raised to believe he was all-important, and his inability to see further than his own selfish desires repelled her as nothing had ever done before.

"Leave me alone!" she shouted angrily, uncaring that she was a spectacle for the other people in the lobby.

Something changed in Somner's eyes. His face, always the picture of stoicism, turned a mottled red. His eyes narrowed, and his lips grew taut. Then his arms shot forward, his hands grasping her shoulders tightly as he drew her close.

"I always get what I want!" he declared.

Cassandra tried to pull away but could not. So instead she tried not to feel the pain from his hands as she looked at him. She saw the truth of his words reflected in his features, and at the same time vowed that she would never become his property.

"Let go of me," she hissed.

Somner's response was a tightening of his hands on her shoulders. "You will be mine!"

She tried to pull away again, but he squeezed harder. Then, from out of nowhere, a man grasped Somner's wrists. Somner winced painfully, and Cassandra's eyes widened with recognition . . . and something else. It was the man from the restaurant.

"I believe the lady was trying to get into this elevator," the man said, releasing Somner's wrists.

As soon as Somner turned to face the stranger, Cassandra fled into the elevator and pressed the button. Before the doors closed, she saw that the man was facing Somner without a trace of fear. When the doors finally closed, Cassandra leaned back and took several deep breaths.

For a moment she thought she was experiencing the

aftereffects of the shocking confrontation, but she soon realized that the chaos in her mind was not caused by Somner's actions.

No, it was far from that: In the brief seconds when she'd looked into the eyes of the stranger, her entire being had reacted to him. It was more than being rescued, much more.

When he'd spoken to Somner, the rich timbre of his voice had struck a chord within her, and her mind and body had resonated powerfully. The strength she'd glimpsed in the man's face and the powerful aura surrounding him had shaken her immensely.

Cassandra didn't hear the bell for her floor. Only when the door opened, did she realize she was at her destination. Shaking from too many thoughts rampaging through her mind, Cassandra walked toward the security of her office.

Once she was safely behind her door, she sat on the brown suede couch and tried to organize her thoughts. So much had happened so quickly. She had learned the true character of the man she had almost married and was grateful she had run away three months before. If not . . . But Cassandra wouldn't let herself think of that.

Who was the person I had lunch with? How could I have thought myself to be in love with him? But, even as she asked herself these questions, another sharper question reared its head. *How could I have not known what he was really like?* And suddenly she was remembering the way Somner's eyes had turned dangerous. She realized he had fully expected her to give in to his demands without a thought for herself.

He said he loved me.

"How could he!" she answered herself aloud.

A shiver raced along her spine. She had thought she was doing the right thing in telling Somner about her feelings.

She liked him a great deal; she had even thought herself in love with him. She had wanted to make him understand her needs and show him that he was important to her, important enough for her to make sure they were not making a mistake.

But in the last hour, she had come to realize the truth of the matter. Somner Barwell did not care about her emotions —only his. And in that frightening moment by the elevator, she had caught a glimpse of just how far he would go to get what he wanted.

Facing horses couldn't be any worse than facing him, Cassandra told herself.

Yet even as she thought of Somner, she thought of the man who had come to her aid. *Who is he?* she wondered, as the stranger's face floated before her eyes.

The man had stood a good two inches taller than Somner, and his broad shoulders had dwarfed him. A full head of wavy brown hair had set off a startlingly handsome face. But it wasn't a movie star's good looks; rather, he had a rugged quality of inherent strength.

Intuitively Cassandra knew that if she had not run away, if she had stayed to meet him, something would have happened between them, something would have had to happen. Understanding that, Cassandra was glad she had run. Her life was just beginning.

Cassandra could not brook any distractions. She had to prove her abilities, not only to her father, but to herself as well. The stranger would be much more than just a distraction.

Work! Get to work! she told herself. Rising from the couch, Cassandra went to her desk and sat down. For an endless time, she stared at the sheets of figures laid out before her, but her eyes would not focus. Then she glanced at her watch. It was two o'clock. In another hour she would be going to her father's office to meet the general manager of the ranch.

Knowing this, she reached across the desk and picked up the file folder that Personnel had sent over the day before. The tab of the folder had two words on it—Kirk North.

Opening it, Cassandra began to read the detailed history of the man she would be working with for the next twelve months. A man she knew would resent her presence, and her involvement.

Chapter Four

After the unexpected encounter in the lobby, Kirk had gone for a walk to cool off. He'd never thought himself the hero type, but when, coincidentally, he'd seen the woman from the restaurant trying to get away from the man, he had been unable to stop himself from helping her.

Even now, a half hour later, as he waited for the elevator to reach his floor, he could not rid himself of the vision of the beautiful woman. The man had been angry, but when Kirk had stared into his eyes, he'd seen the anger fade. When Kirk had released him, he'd stood silently until the man turned and left the building. Then he'd done the same thing.

He'd walked for twenty minutes, clearing his mind and preparing himself for his meeting with Gregory Leeds. Yet no matter how hard he tried, he could not erase the image in his mind of her face as she fought the man. There had been no fear on her features, only anger. Kirk had liked that, too.

He'd liked everything about the woman he would never see again.

When he got out of the elevator, he found himself before a large Plexiglas reception desk, complete with a pretty receptionist.

"Did you have a good lunch, Mr. North?" she asked.

"Unusual," he replied with a slow smile.

"But interesting?"

"To say the least," Kirk added dryly.

"Mr. Leeds is waiting. He said to send you in as soon as you returned from lunch."

"Thank you," Kirk said as he strode past her desk and through the wide entrance to Leeds International's executive offices.

He walked directly to the end of the hallway and knocked on the frosted double doors before opening them and going inside.

"Good afternoon, Mr. North," Leeds' secretary, Elizabeth, said, rising and motioning him toward yet another door. "Mr. Leeds is expecting you." Saying this, she went to that door and opened it.

Kirk nodded and entered Gregory Leeds' office. As he had been on his three previous visits here, Kirk was startled by the opulence. The office was huge. It was a corner office with two full walls of windows looking out on the city. A large teak desk dominated the center of the office, and Gregory Leeds sat at it.

Off to one side was a gleaming chrome and wood wet bar, and strewn in an almost casual fashion were several chairs and a couch.

"Hello, Kirk. Enjoy lunch?" Gregory Leeds asked as he rose from his chair and went to greet Kirk with a firm handshake

Rather than get into what happened, Kirk nodded. "Very much." It was true, too, he realized; very true.

"Care for a drink?"

"No, thank you. What I need is to find out what's going on." While he spoke, he held Leeds' stare with his own.

"At least we didn't offer you a raise this year," Leeds only half jested.

"I had expected to be fired."

Gregory Leeds nodded his head thoughtfully. "I can appreciate that, Kirk. I have a large number of employees working for me. Some are good, some aren't. But there are a few who are better than good. Those people are the ones I call the achievers. They're loyal and strive to do not only the best, but more."

When Leeds paused, Kirk held back his reaction to the flattery.

"You're one of the men in that category. Kirk, I've built a large business on my ability to pick the right man for the right job—"

"And the right man will be overseeing me?" Kirk cut in, not wanting to hear any more whitewash.

For a second after he'd spoken, Kirk saw that his boss was uncomfortable.

Gregory Leeds laughed. It was a good clean sound that caught Kirk off guard. "I deserved that. Kirk, you are doing the best job possible at Twin Rivers. Murray already told you so, but I'll reiterate it for you. I am extremely pleased with your handling of the ranch—period; nothing more can be added."

"Mr. Leeds, may I ask you a question?"

"Fire away."

"If you're satisfied with my work, even though Twin

Rivers is running in the red, why is a vice president of Leeds International coming to look over my shoulder?'' Although he knew better than to be this blunt, Kirk didn't really care. He wanted at least one answer to what was becoming a giant-size crossword puzzle.

"You don't pull punches, do you? Very well," Gregory Leeds said, "have a seat."

Kirk went to the nearest couch and sat as Leeds did the same in a chair across from him. When they were both settled, Leeds crossed one leg over the other.

"The vice president I'm sending with you is my daughter. Kirk, I find myself faced with a rather unique problem. My daughter, Cassandra, has decided that she wants to be a business executive."

"That's not unusual today," Kirk replied after recovering from his initial shock.

"No, it's not, except for the fact that Cassandra turned twenty-seven two weeks ago and has never worked a day in her life."

Kirk tried to keep his face expressionless but could not stop the sudden arching of his eyebrows. "And now she wants to work?"

"It was a perfect match! Perfect! She was supposed—" Gregory began but stopped himself. "But she picked up this . . . bug about wanting to prove herself. She wants to work for a year. At the end of that period, well, I wouldn't worry about it," he said offhandedly.

Kirk was even more confused than before. Men as powerful as Gregory Leeds do not unburden themselves to their employees, not at least, without a good motive. "So you made her a vice president?"

"In a manner of speaking. She has no experience. I

couldn't let her work in a position of any importance without that experience. But she is my daughter, and she wants to prove herself.''

"And Twin Rivers is unimportant enough to let her do that?'' Kirk asked sarcastically. "I'm sorry, Mr. Leeds, but I take my work seriously, even if you think the ranch is a toy.''

A momentary flash of anger showed on Leeds' face, but he managed to control himself. "I've fired people for less than that,'' he warned.

"But not for failing to make a profit?'' he asked dryly.

"That too, as a matter of fact, if the failure was because they didn't do their jobs properly. You, on the other hand, besides having a tricky temper, do your job well. And I do not regard Twin Rivers as a toy. In fact, I regard the ranch as a very important part of Leeds International.''

Kirk eased off. Something about the way the chairman of the board spoke made him retreat a little. Sitting back on the couch, he waited silently, ever wary.

"May I get back on track?'' Leeds smiled as Kirk nodded. "I intend to have Cassandra spend a year at Twin Rivers, getting firsthand experience and learning about business. I expect you to continue on as you have been, running the ranch and doing your usual excellent job.''

"What you're saying is that your daughter will be a figurehead, a vice president in name only, and I will continue to make all decisions?''

"Basically. You would make the majority of decisions, especially on important matters. Cassandra would be the nominal head of the ranch, as a vice president of Leeds International.''

Kirk had been listening intently to Gregory Leeds' voice. Behind the words, Kirk detected something else, a faint echo of desperation, perhaps even hopelessness. Kirk understood then that he was being asked to baby-sit.

In the back of Kirk's mind, though, was the troublesome thought that if Leeds was sending anyone at all, even his inexperienced daughter, there must be a reason. And, he wondered, was that reason part of a dissatisfaction with Kirk's performance at the ranch?

"As I see it," Kirk began, choosing his words carefully, "I have no choice. You're couching an order in the form of a request."

"True, but I have a good reason."

"Yes?"

"My daughter is one of the two most important people in the world to me, but I don't want her pandered to. Kirk, we've only met a few times, but I've watched you since Leeds took over Twin Rivers. You didn't come to me for your job; I went to you. And quite honestly, there's no one in my organization who would stand up to her, or to me, the way you do. That's why I chose Twin Rivers for Cassie."

"How can you be certain I won't . . . pander to her?"

"Do you want a raise?"

"When I earn it."

"That's why!"

"What happens at the end of the year if she wants to stay at Twin Rivers? Do I move on?"

Gregory Leeds' face, sober until then, perked up. "No. You'll have to trust me, Kirk, but I can promise you there's absolutely no chance of Cassandra staying on. In fact, I doubt she'll last out the year."

Kirk, again hearing a strange undertone in Leeds' voice, knew he had no choice other than to quit. "All right, Mr. Leeds."

As if to emphasize the end of the conversation, Gregory

Leeds' intercom buzzed. Rising swiftly, Leeds went to the desk and pressed the button. "Yes?"

"Cassandra is here," his secretary informed him.

"Send her in," Gregory Leeds said as his eyes locked with Kirk North's.

Cassandra strode boldly into her father's office, looking neither right nor left. She smiled, but her smile did not conceal the petulant set of her face as she stared at her father. "Is your cowboy here yet?" she asked sarcastically.

Cassandra's father held his features immobile for a moment before he favored her with a knowing nod. "As a matter of fact, Mr. North is seated right behind you."

Cassandra stiffened involuntarily but forced her suddenly taut lips into a shadowy smile as she turned. The smile froze the instant she recognized the handsome man who was gazing at her with deep brown eyes. Her heart seemed to stop beating; her throat refused to allow air into her lungs. She stared at him for endless seconds until, at last, she broke free of her trance. "You . . ." she whispered, unable to say more.

At her side, Gregory Leeds looked from Cassandra to Kirk, a clearly puzzled expression on his face.

"I guess *this cowboy* started his job a few hours early," Kirk said, free now of his earlier sensation of loss, which these first crass words of hers had effectively shattered.

When she had entered the office, he had been taken by surprise; Cassandra Leeds was the woman he had never expected to see again. His body had gone tense with recognition, but the tension had changed into something else after she'd spoken. Before she'd turned to face him, he knew the attraction he felt for her was wrong. It was an attraction to surface beauty. Kirk realized that Cassandra Leeds was too sarcastic and callow a woman for him to consider special.

Standing, Kirk cut off his thoughts and walked toward her. When he was three feet away, he extended his hand.

Cassandra watched him walk and felt the powerful aura that surrounded him. Unknowingly she had caught her lower lip with her teeth in a nervous gesture. When he offered her his hand, she slowly reached out to take it.

The instant their hands touched, Cassandra experienced a rushing flow of heat that spread upward along her arm before expanding to suffuse through her entire body. Their hands stayed together, and their eyes locked for a long drawn-out moment.

Only when he released her hand did sanity return. "I. . . . Forgive me, Mr. North, I didn't really mean what I said."

"And I wish I could believe that. But I'll accept a thank-you for what happened earlier."

Cassandra could still feel the heat of his skin on hers, although her hand was free and hanging at her side. Moistening her lips with the tip of her tongue, Cassandra nodded her head. "Thank you," she whispered.

"Would somebody like to tell me what's going on?" Gregory Leeds asked.

Cassandra glanced at her father, about to speak, but Kirk spoke first.

"Your daughter was having some trouble with a man downstairs. I helped her out."

Cassandra saw the next question coming from her father and knew she did not want to get involved with that now. "It was nothing," she told him. Then she turned back to

Kirk. "I do hope you'll forgive me for being so boorish. We'll be spending a good deal of time together."

"I'm well aware of that," Kirk said tersely.

"Well, now that you've both been ah . . . formally introduced, may I suggest that we get down to business?"

Both Cassandra and Kirk nodded and followed Gregory Leeds to the far side of the office, where three chairs surrounded a table already set with cups, saucers, and a coffeepot.

Eight hours after meeting Kirk North, Cassandra sank into the steaming tub and tried to rid herself of worry and unease. Her bags were packed and waiting by the front door, but her mind was not yet ready for this next step in her life.

Resting her head on the gilded edge of the large tub, Cassandra forced her muscles to relax and allow the hot water to work its special magic on them.

Her eyes would not stay closed, however, because when they were, *his* face floated before her. His eyes burned deeply into hers with unspoken accusation as the memory of the afternoon's fiasco rose fresh in her mind.

Her humiliation at the first meeting with Kirk North seemed hotter than the water she lay in, and she could still feel the way her cheeks had flamed from her initial faux pas in her father's office.

She had entered his office in a cultivated mood of aggression and defensiveness. Cassandra had believed that she must establish her authority immediately in order to survive the coming year. She had been foolish and careless, though, in expecting to find a typical cowboy whom she wanted to impress with her power, especially after having read his personnel file. Instead she'd found the one person who had already proven that he was far from her own preconceived notion of a cowboy.

Cassandra remembered her father's funny smile after she'd made her thoughtless entering remark. He had liked the situation she'd put herself in. Cassandra knew he had sensed that the first round of victory went to him.

Not yet, Father! she promised herself.

The rest of the afternoon had taken on the aspect of a marathon: Her father had gone over all the details of her new position so that Kirk North would clearly understand who she was and why she was going to Twin Rivers.

Whenever she'd glanced at Kirk, his face had been devoid of expression. In fact, after the first few words he'd spoken to her, his face had become an emotionless mask.

But what was even more disconcerting was the way he'd spoken to her. Whenever he referred to her, it was in the third person. She had wanted to yell at him but knew she could not. Instead she'd reinforced her determination to be strong.

Closing her eyes, Cassandra tried to think of something else but failed.

"I believe that takes care of everything," Gregory Leeds had said with a smile. "I'll expect detailed reports monthly," he had added to Cassandra.

"Of course," she'd replied.

Then her father had turned to Kirk. "All the arrangements have been made for the new stud?"

"Yes, sir. I'll be finalizing them on the way back. The papers have been authenticated and certified by the Appaloosa Horse Club and by the Breeders Association."

"I expect good news at foaling time."

"Plan on it," Kirk had said. Then he'd stood and looked at her. "Ma'am, I'll see you at the airport, seven fifteen."

"I'll be there," Cassandra had said, forcing a perfectly formed but patently false smile to counter his all too intense gaze.

"I'm sure of that." Then he had turned back to her father and shaken his hand before leaving the office.

When the door had closed behind him, her father had fixed her with a withering stare. "That was a poor way to start things off."

Cassandra, her defenses as yet not rebuilt, lowered her eyes. "I know."

"It's not too late, Cassie. You don't have to go through with this."

Cassandra had raised her eyes, and a slow smile spread across her lips. Until her father had spoken, she'd felt extremely vulnerable, but his invitation to give up was the very thing she needed to strengthen her resolve.

"But I do, Father, and I will!" With that, Cassandra had stood. "Will I see you later, at home?"

"If not tonight, I will certainly be there to see you off in the morning."

"As usual," Cassandra said to the bathroom ceiling as she opened her eyes and chased away the afternoon's memory. Her father had always been a busy man—too busy to give her the time she had always wanted, especially since her accident. She had wanted to spend her last night in New York with him and her mother, but as usual Gregory Leeds was too busy to have dinner with his only daughter.

So she and her mother had eaten a quiet meal, and then she'd finished packing her bags. After that, she'd gone for a short walk, knowing that she might not be back for a year.

Cassandra stood, and the water cascaded like a waterfall from her tall lithe frame. Fifteen minutes later she was dry and in a soft cotton nightgown, sitting on the edge of her bed.

Glancing at the clock, she saw it was almost one A.M. She knew she should try to sleep; she would have to get up in less than five hours. But she didn't feel the least bit tired.

Sleep and Cassandra had become flirting strangers since her father had made his decision. *He won't break me!* she declared to herself, refusing to let herself dwell on the one aspect that frightened her more than anything else in the world—the one thing that would make this job an unending personal hell.

Forcing herself to stop thinking about *that,* Cassandra lay down and turned off the bedside lamp. She closed her eyes and tried to sleep, but instead, Kirk North's handsome face returned to haunt her again.

"No!" she yelled, sitting up and turning on the lamp. The low flood of gentle yellow light helped calm her down, but Kirk's face would not disappear, nor did her body's reaction. Again, as had happened in her father's office, Cassandra felt the heat rising within her.

She remembered the way he had so easily handled Somner, and she remembered, too, the hard, tough way he had stared her would-be-fiancé down. The power that radiated around him was a dangerous thing, Cassandra knew, for she could feel its call even now.

And I have to spend twelve months with him. What will happen? Can I do it? she asked herself.

"I will make it," she promised. Cassandra understood instinctively that she could not allow herself to fall under Kirk North's mesmerizing aura. If she was to be his boss, she had to prove that she could do the job better than he had.

Ranching is just another type of business, she tried to tell herself. She tried, but failed. What was a ranch without horses?

Cassandra shivered. She was nine again, riding along the beautiful green meadow in Long Island. The sun was warm overhead; the large, powerful Thoroughbred beneath her moved at a swift pace.

She remembered her father's proud look, and then . . . "Stop!" she shouted, wrapping her arms around herself to keep from shaking, and to will an end to the memory.

Thankfully Cassandra was able to divert her thoughts away from the past, rescued from that horror by thinking about something no less dangerous but far less frightening —Kirk North.

When she had gone into the meeting with her father and Kirk, she had known that Kirk was not just a cowboy, a fact she had chosen to disregard in making her first power play. She had read his personnel file. Kirk North was a well-educated man who had graduated in the upper ten percent of his class at the University of Arizona. She had been surprised, too, to learn that Kirk had been awarded three medals during his service in Vietnam.

No, Cassandra realized, Kirk North was no cowboy. At last, Cassandra's tired and warring mind could fight no longer, and a few moments later she fell into a light but troubled sleep.

Chapter Five

*C*assandra stifled the yawn that threatened to escape and gazed from the corner of her eye at the handsome man seated next to her. They had been together for five and a half hours, and in all, he'd spoken to her three times.

She sensed his dislike of her, tried to accept it, but could not. She had apologized to him yesterday and had been determined to be on her best behavior today, having realized belatedly one very important fact. If she was to succeed in her quest for freedom and self-validation, Kirk North would play a major role. Without him and his knowledge, she would never be able to do her job.

But his antagonism had flared as soon as she'd gotten out of the limousine at the airport. His antagonism and that "something else" about him. As it happened, yesterday her entire being had reacted to him. But she'd forced herself to remain poised, her emotions hidden.

No sooner had the chauffeur begun to take her bags from the trunk than she'd seen his amused smile. "Have you ever lived on a ranch?" he'd asked.

"No."

"There isn't much call for a large wardrobe," he'd told her, his eyes sweeping over the abundance of her luggage.

"Mr. North, I haven't brought a large wardrobe," she'd responded in icy tones.

"Yes, ma'am," he'd said without losing his infuriating grin.

The next time they talked was when they boarded the plane. In the aisle, Kirk had nodded his head and offered her the window seat.

"How gallant," she'd said. Only she hadn't meant to speak the words aloud, just to herself.

"Not really," Kirk had responded, "I need the aisle to stretch my legs."

Nonplussed, Cassandra refused to look at him as she went to her seat. But as she tried to hide her embarrassment, a different type of warmth rose in her cheeks, sped on its way by the simple action of his hand touching the bare skin of her elbow, guiding her to her seat. With his touch had come a tingling that, a half a heartbeat later, had engulfed her body.

She tried but could not control her reaction to that lightest of touches.

Thankfully for Cassandra, the plane had taken off on schedule and breakfast had been served. Breakfast, as everything else had been since she'd gotten to the airport, was a silent affair that continued long after the food trays had been removed, and Kirk had opened the *New York Times*.

Two hours into the flight Cassandra had broken the

silence Kirk had imposed. "Could we talk?" she'd asked. She'd had to wait a full minute for his reply.

"About?"

"Our situation."

"Go ahead."

Cassandra had wanted to scream. For the two hours she'd been sitting next to him, the aura that surrounded him like an all-encompassing umbrella had grated unmercifully on her nerves. Yet Kirk had seemed oblivious of her presence.

"I realize you don't like me," she'd begun, but he cut her off.

"You're supposed to be my new boss, Miss Leeds, not a mind reader. You don't know whether or not I like you."

His voice had had the flinty edge of decisiveness. She had seen it, too, in the brown depths of his eyes when he turned to emphasize his words. For an instant, Cassandra was caught within his gaze and found herself fighting the trap her emotions were leading her toward—a pitfall that could only end in disaster. Concentrating with all her might, Cassandra broke the spell.

"Whatever . . . but it is my job to see that Twin Rivers makes a profit this year. Without your cooperation—"

"I'm the general manager, Miss Leeds. As such, I'm paid a rather high salary to cooperate with you."

"Then why are you treating me like this?"

"I don't know what you mean."

"Like hell you don't!" And with that, Cassandra had turned from him to look out at the blue sky that went on forever. She had felt, too, the first pangs of a loneliness that she knew could only get worse. *I will survive!*

When the announcement of their landing came over the loudspeaker, Cassandra spoke again. "How long is the trip from Denver to Phoenix?" she asked.

Kirk's brow furrowed for a moment. "About twenty-four hours."

"What?"

"Miss Leeds, we aren't going to Twin Rivers today."

"We aren't? . . . What are you talking about?"

"We're going to Wyoming to sign the papers for a new stud."

"Whose idea was that?" she demanded, thrown off stride by this news. "My father's?"

"Arrangements were made two weeks ago. Weren't you told?" he asked, surprised by her lack of knowledge and apparent anger.

"Apparently not."

"The ranch's plane is at the Denver airport, and we'll leave just as soon as possible. You know," Kirk ventured thoughtfully, ignoring her hostility, "this will be a good opportunity to see one of the things that I hope will help Twin Rivers show a profit."

"Why can't the papers be mailed and signed?"

Kirk almost succeeded in hiding his brief flash of annoyance. "They could have been, especially since I know and trust the breeder. But I've never seen the stallion, and I learned a long time ago never to sign anything without seeing what I'm getting first. Sometimes, no matter how good a stud's papers are, you can look at him and know he isn't the right one. But I think he'll be fine. In fact, two of our ranch hands are meeting us there with a horse trailer to take him back to Twin Rivers."

"All of that for a . . . horse?" she asked, not able to keep the disbelief out of her voice.

Kirk studied her beautiful face for several long seconds while he held his irritation in check. "A stud, Miss Leeds, is not just a horse. A good stud ensures that a herd will flourish. A good stud also brings the price of foals higher.''

''I suppose the female doesn't count in the greater scheme of things?''

''Mare, Miss Leeds, mare. Brood mares count, Miss Leeds, but the value for the type of horse we breed is in the stud.''

''Of course,'' Cassandra replied tersely.

Hearing the sibilant tones in her answer brought home to Kirk that he was as much to blame in this war of nerves as she. He was angry about the loss of his freedom as general manager and foreman, although Gregory Leeds had assured him he had not lost anything, that he was just a baby-sitter. And combined with that news were the memories of his first reactions to her in the restaurant. He knew he was venting his frustrations.

Yesterday he had seen a very special woman, the kind whom he would have chased to the ends of the earth. But no sooner had this happened than his illusions had been broken, and he'd been forced to see that in reality she was a spoiled and shallow rich girl about to play with her daddy's money.

Kirk knew that Cassandra Leeds would soon learn many lessons in life, for no matter who you were, or who your father was, if you didn't gain the respect of the people on the ranch, your life would be a lonely series of days, and the ranch itself would flounder. Cowboys were a different breed of men. There were always jobs for them, and it was easier to move on than to work for someone you didn't respect.

For a cowboy that was the rule, but not for a foreman and general manager. And for Kirk, Twin Rivers was an important job. Without it, his goals would be set back.

Although he tried to rationalize his emotions, he could not rid himself of the feelings that continued to battle within him. He could not deny—and he had tried to since yesterday afternoon—that he was attracted to Cassandra in a way he had never been to another woman.

Kirk knew the kind of poison a woman like Cassandra Leeds was to a man like himself. And added to that was the fact that she was the boss's daughter.

When the plane landed in Denver, Kirk led Cassandra to the baggage counter, where they claimed her five suitcases and his one leather traveling bag. With Cassandra, a porter, and his baggage cart in tow, he left the main terminal and walked the quarter-mile to the private hangar where the ranch's twin engine Beechcraft waited.

While the luggage was loaded, Kirk left to file the flight plan. When he returned and went to the plane, Cassandra looked around. "Where's the pilot?"

"You're looking at him," Kirk stated. "That was one of my money-saving cuts."

"I should have guessed," she whispered, still looking at him.

"Would you like to see my papers?" he asked.

"No," she replied as she stepped onto the small passenger step and entered the plane.

They waited on the runway until the tower gave them permission to taxi, and soon they were airborne. An hour later they were flying over yet another range of mountains.

"Have you ever flown in a small craft?"

"Not one with propellers, or ones that go so slowly," she replied, thinking of the many times she'd flown in her friends' private jets.

"Naturally. But at least this gives you a chance to enjoy the scenery."

It wasn't his tone this time, but his words that made her look at him. "Did I hear you right? Did you say I would enjoy the scenery?" she asked, her voice filled with incredulity.

Kirk set the controls and put the plane on autopilot before turning to look at her. Once again her beauty tore at him, striking deep within him and making him want to reach out, shake her, and tell her about the realities of life. "Would you prefer that we didn't talk unless it was about business?"

Cassandra, her pulse racing with the intensity of his stare, felt the tension in the air as if it were a thick and tenaciously clinging fog. "No," she whispered, her mouth dry and parched for no reason.

"You're a jet-setter, you've been all over the world, Miss Leeds, but have you ever been out west?"

"California," she replied after moistening her lips.

"Look out there," he said, motioning toward the ground. "Look at the mountains; look at the harsh beauty of the land. It takes a lot to live here, and it takes more to conquer it."

Cassandra followed his pointing finger, and her breath caught at the magnificence of the endless mountain range. Although it was late spring, snow still covered the mountain peaks in startling contrast to the lush green slopes beneath them. Kirk's words echoed in her mind until she began to understand what he was saying.

As she looked at the bountiful vista spread out below her, her own desire to make a success out of her life returned forcefully. Without taking her eyes from the scene, she spoke in a low, intense voice. "I intend to do just that, Mr. North. I intend to live here. But I don't want to conquer the land, just make the ranch work."

"They're one and the same thing, Miss Leeds," Kirk said, surprised at the sound of determination in her voice.

"Can we stop the formality? My name is Cassandra."

For the first time since she'd met him, Kirk gave her a full smile. She wished he hadn't. The crow's-feet at the corners of his eyes spread outward into his cheeks. Cassandra realized she had never before met a man like Kirk North, never.

"Okay," he said.

"Kirk?"

"Yes?"

"How much longer?" Cassandra asked.

"A half hour. After we land in Sheridan, we'll go to the ranch and look over the stud. We'll fly out tomorrow morning and should be at Twin Rivers by mid-afternoon."

"What is Sheridan?" she asked.

Kirk favored her with a sideways glance. "A small town by your standards."

"That should be interesting," she commented, looking out at yet another oncoming mountain range.

"The Big Horns," Kirk told her as he shut off the autopilot and took back control of the plane.

Once Kirk had made the arrangements for servicing the plane, they went to the waiting rental car and, with only one of her five suitcases, she and Kirk drove out to the ranch. "The Broken Spur," Kirk had told her.

How quaint, she had wanted to say, but had held back the remark, hoping to keep the tension between them light. Cassandra knew that Kirk was just barely tolerating her, and she was starting to understand that he had every right to do so.

She was now his boss, but she knew nothing about

ranching, a fact he was well aware of. *I'll change that soon enough,* she told herself as she concentrated on the passing scenery. The mountains that bordered the road were indeed formidable, and the rough green vegetation seemed less dense than it had appeared from the air.

"What is that stuff?" she asked.

"What stuff?"

"The small bushes."

"Buffalo grass," Kirk replied.

"I thought buffalos were extinct," Cassandra replied immediately.

Kirk waited a patient moment before answering her. "Buffalo grass is the basic vegetation of Wyoming. It's what the range animals graze on. This part of the country is a bit hostile to lawn grass."

Cassandra heard the undertone of condescension, but ignored it. "Is that what we have in Arizona?"

"Not quite, but not too far off, either. The open ranges aren't exactly what you thought they'd be, are they?" As he asked the question, he tried to see her face.

Cassandra smiled. "Nothing is like the movies; I've learned that lesson already. Tell me about the stud," she requested, instantly regretting her demand.

Kirk talked about it, but he concentrated more on the road than on Cassandra's face, which she was grateful for, because as he spoke, her body tensed. She couldn't help it: whenever anyone talked about horses, she had the same reaction.

She heard a different tone in Kirk's voice than she was used to when people spoke about animals. His voice was almost reverent, and he seemed to give the animal human qualities. Strangely it was not unpleasant.

When he finished talking, he slowed the car and turned

off the main road onto a smaller one-lane blacktop. "The Broken Spur begins here," he said, pointing to a small sign on the side.

"How large is it?" she asked.

"About fifteen thousand acres," he informed her as they crested a hill. When they started down, Cassandra saw the ranch spread out beneath them. There were several large buildings, two barns, and a half dozen small corrals.

"It's a big place," she commented.

"About average," Kirk replied as he stopped the car. "The main house is directly ahead. That long building off to the side is the bunkhouse, and that," he said, pointing to a corral on the opposite side of the buildings, "is our new stud."

When he finished speaking, he started driving again, but Cassandra's eyes were locked on the corral. It was at least a quarter-mile away, and from this distance, the horse looked small and safe.

A few moments later Kirk pulled the car to a stop before a large barn and got out. He came around the car and, as Cassandra opened her door, offered her his hand. "Watch your step," he advised.

Now she knew why he had looked at her so strangely at the airport when he'd asked her if she wanted to change and she had decided not to. Kirk had put on a pair of faded jeans, cowboy boots, and a lightweight cotton shirt.

"You might be more comfortable," he'd told her.

Cassandra had decided to wear the dress she had on, along with the three-inch heels that complemented it so perfectly. But beneath her feet was only muddy, rocky earth, and her footing was treacherous, to say the least.

Refusing to acknowledge her error and give him a sense of victory, Cassandra smiled, released the hand that was turning her own to a burning cinder, and followed him as best she could.

Within seconds after leaving the car, Cassandra forgot her difficulty in walking, as the varied smells of the ranch struck her. She smelled a myriad of things—earth, hay— but most pervasive of all was the concentrated scent of horses.

Unable to stop it, tentacles of fear infiltrated her mind, making her unsteady walk even more unsteady. By sheer dint of her willpower, Cassandra forced herself to stand straight and not allow her shivering to turn into full tremors.

She concentrated on the man ahead of her, seeing only his broad back. But even the powerful aura of his masculinity did not help.

Halfway to the corral, a gruff voice called out to them. Kirk turned, a smile on his face. "Hello, Hank," he said as he shook the man's hand.

"'lo Kirk, been waiting for you." As he spoke, he glanced at Cassandra, his face open and questioning.

"Cassandra Leeds, meet Hank Lomax, owner of the Broken Spur."

Cassandra took the large hand he extended to her. "A pleasure, Miss Cassandra," he said in a heavy western accent. Then he glanced at her feet and saw what she was wearing. "Perhaps you'd like to wait in the house. Wouldn't want you to twist one of those purty ankles. Besides," he added with an understanding smile, "you'll get awfully dirty at the corral."

"So I've been noticing. But thank you anyway, I'd like to go along."

"Sure thing, just watch out for the rocks; they can be tricky."

Cassandra nodded, trying to squeeze out a smile she

didn't feel. She started after the men once again, but when they were twenty feet from the corral, Cassandra's legs refused to move as fear gripped her in its paralyzing vise. She stared at the corral, and at the suddenly gigantic stallion, whose pinkish flaring nostrils and wide dark eyes, riveted her to the spot. When the stallion whinnied loudly, she shivered again. "Kirk," she called, forcing her voice to not break.

Kirk turned and saw her standing still. "Need help?" he asked.

"I . . . I think I'll wait by the car; I really am getting filthy." The moment the words were out, she saw the disappointment on his face. His eyes, which had been so friendly since their conversation in the plane, went cold.

"We'll be done in a little while," he told her as he turned around and continued on to the corral.

Cassandra stood there for several seconds before gaining the strength to move and make her way slowly and carefully back to the car.

"She doesn't seem to be your type," Hank commented a moment after they reached the corral. "City girl and all. Sure doesn't like to get that purty outfit dirty, does she?"

"How could you tell?" Kirk asked, unable to keep the tightness out of his voice.

"I got to admit she is a looker though."

"And spoiled rotten. No, Hank, you're right, she's not my type."

"Then who is she?" Hank Lomax asked, eyeing Kirk carefully.

"The boss's daughter. I'm baby-sitting," Kirk stated as he turned to look at the stallion. He realized it was truer than he'd wanted to admit. Gregory Leeds had been honest with him: He was playing nursemaid to Cassandra.

"That may not be too bad a job."

"You want it?" Kirk asked angrily.

Hank just smiled. "No, thanks. I'm happy doing what I do best," he said, nodding pointedly at the stallion.

"Fifteen hands. Not bad," Kirk said.

"He's a handsome one, Kirk."

"That he is," Kirk replied as he studied the stallion.

Appaloosas were pure riding horses. They had been bred for just that, and Kirk saw that this powerful stallion was no exception. Its conformation was perfect, its color exactly what the books said. Dark grayish-black spots proliferated along a silky white body. It was easy to see in a single glance that the horse had the prerequisite amount of Arabian bloodlines.

"He's a beauty," Kirk commented.

"And he'll sire a hell of a good line of riding horses," Hank added.

"Why don't we sign those papers so I can give you your check."

"Fine. Your men called 'bout an hour ago. Said they got held up by some roadwork. Won't be here till dark."

"No problem, Hank. Just tell them to load up and give me a call before they take off. We'll be at the Best Western."

"One room or two?" Hank asked with another smile.

"I wish it were two motels."

"Look, son," Hank said, his face serious, "I've known you for a few years, and I've never heard you talk about anyone like that. Why are you so down on her?"

"Ready to sign those papers?" he asked, disregarding the question that the man who had hired him nine years ago when he'd finished college had asked so perceptively.

Twenty minutes later Kirk returned to the car.

"Finished?" Cassandra asked.

"Uh-huh," Kirk replied.

"Now where?" she asked, hating the way Kirk was staring straight ahead. Once again tension filled the air. Cassandra hated that, too.

"Don't worry, you won't get dirty. We're going to the motel."

"Kirk," Cassandra began, wanting to apologize for what had happened yet refusing to be forced into explaining her actions to him. "You could have told me why you suggested I change."

"Am I going to have to spend the next year explaining everything that happens? Why not try to use the brain you were born with? You're not in New York anymore!" he snapped, starting the car as he uttered the last word.

They made the drive back to Sheridan in total silence, and when Kirk registered at the motel, he did it quickly and efficiently. They had rooms side by side on the second floor, and Kirk handed her the key and started off.

"At least have the courtesy to wait for me," Cassandra whispered angrily. "This suitcase is heavy."

"Yes, ma'am," Kirk replied sarcastically. Reaching the elevator, he leaned against the wall and waited for her to follow with the large suitcase.

He let her struggle with it, knowing that if he went to help her, he would be giving in. When she reached him, he pressed for the elevator. A moment later the door hissed open, and he stepped inside, again waiting for her to hoist the suitcase and follow him.

They both looked straight ahead at the silver door until the elevator doors opened on their floor. Kirk again took the lead and walked halfway down the hall to their rooms. As he put his key into the lock, he heard Cassandra do the same.

Before he could open the door, Cassandra spoke. Her tone was light, her voice sweet. "Kirk?"

Kirk turned, his face set in a scowl, his eyebrows raised, waiting.

"You're a real bastard, but you're not going to scare me off," she said in a flat, low voice.

"Yes, ma'am," he replied. Then he went into his room and closed the door.

Cassandra turned off the water and stepped from the shower stall into the steam-filled bathroom. Her nerves were still tight, and her mind was as unsettled as ever. Her rage was seething and strong, and she dried herself so roughly that her skin turned an angry shade of crimson.

"How dare he!" she yelled to the moisture-filmed mirror. "He has no right to treat me like this!"

Her breasts rose and fell forcefully under the power of her emotions. "He doesn't know me! But he will!" she promised.

Then she left the bathroom, stopping when she saw her shoes lying on the floor near the bed. The very expensive pair of heels had been ruined by the mud, and Cassandra knew they would never be fit to wear again.

"Damn him!" she yelled to the shoes. And as it had happened on the plane, another wave of loneliness descended on her, capturing her within its cruelly taunting hold.

I need him if I'm going to make it. Without his help, his knowledge of ranching, I don't stand a chance, she told herself, trying in vain to find some vestige of control.

But it was hard, for Cassandra felt as she had never felt before. She was in the middle of a strange place, akin to a foreign country. There was nowhere to turn, no one to turn to, and nowhere to go. She had only herself, for the man she was with obviously despised her.

What am I doing here? Just then there was a knock on her door. Securing the towel around her she went to it. "Yes?"

"May I speak with you for a moment?" came Kirk's voice.

The anger that had fled at the onslaught of her loneliness returned the instant she heard his voice. Without thinking, she opened the door. In the flash of time it took for the door to open completely, she saw that he was dressed in a pair of gray slacks and wore a deep blue blazer. His dark hair, wet and combed back, was the color of midnight. "What?"

"Dinner," he said, his eyes never leaving her face.

"What for?"

"To eat."

"After the way you treated me? What the hell do you think I am?"

"My new boss."

"You have a lot of nerve. You make me feel like I did something wrong just because I don't know your ways. You look down on me, hardly condescending to talk to me, and when you do, all I hear is sarcasm. And now you want to have dinner with me?" she asked incredulously, her anger beginning to fade.

"Yes, ma'am," he replied.

"Stop that!"

"What, apologizing?"

"Calling me ma'am. My name is Cassandra!"

"What about dinner?"

"When?" she asked, realizing she hadn't eaten since breakfast on the plane ten hours before.

"I guess after you get dressed, unless you're going like that?" he said, moving his eyes for the first time to the towel that barely covered her from her breasts to the top of her thighs.

Cassandra's face turned red and she stepped back. "I'll meet you downstairs in a little while," she told him as she started to close the door.

"Yes, ma'am," he said with a slow grin.

When the door was closed, Cassandra leaned against it and took several deep breaths. *Damn his infuriating smile!* But her anger was gone. He had apologized, in a fashion, and for right now she was willing to accept it.

And worse, she realized, too, was the fact that no matter how angry she'd been at him, she wanted to forgive him—but only because she needed him to help with the ranch.

Even as she refused to accept this, Cassandra knew that there was more to her feelings and actions than she cared to admit.

Chapter Six

*C*assandra finished brushing her hair and stepped back to look at herself in the mirror. In the forty minutes since she'd had her strange conversation with Kirk, she'd put the time to good use.

Her long hair was held in place by a large tortoiseshell barrette, keeping the ever errant strands away from her face. She'd used only a small amount of makeup to accent her features, with no base and just a hint of blush on her cheeks; the lipstick was a dark peach shade that complemented her complexion. Her eyes were done in an understated way with only a glimmer of liner accenting the soft green shadow. Her naturally long eyelashes had an even coat of mascara, and that, she had determined, was enough makeup for Sheridan, Wyoming.

She'd chosen her outfit with care, trying to blend in with the environment. The pale green dress was simple and stylish, falling smoothly to just below her knees and secured at the waist by a contrasting tan elastic belt that matched her saddle tan heels. The only jewelry she wore was a thin bracelet, simple hoop earrings, and the single golden S-chain necklace she never took off.

You won't find any fault tonight, she told the smiling image of Kirk North that hovered in her thoughts.

With that, Cassandra picked up her purse and started from the room, hoping they would make it through dinner in a civil manner. Yet with that thought, a strange feeling of anticipation mixed with the uncertainty of the unknown, making her wonder just what she was expecting to happen tonight.

Kirk nursed his barely touched drink. He had been waiting at the small bar for a half hour, and during that time, he had never stopped thinking of Cassandra.

Every moment he spent with her was like slow torture. He hated what she represented, even as he desired the woman she was. She was a chameleon, he realized. One minute she was a warm and friendly person, the next, as distant as the moon. Yet there had been several times that Kirk had glimpsed something hidden beneath the hard facade Cassandra Leeds wore. But whenever he lowered his guard, she would change back to the hard and shallow city woman he'd met yesterday.

At one point when they'd declared an unspoken truce on the plane, Kirk had begun to let himself open up to her. Then at Hank Lomax's ranch, she'd again showed herself for what she was—a city girl bothered by a little dirt.

But she'd surprised him when they'd returned to the motel, where she had shown him yet another side of her. "You're a real bastard, but you're not going to scare me off," she'd told him. He hadn't smiled at the time, but after he was behind his door, he'd done just that. At least she had a temper, and some spunk to go with it.

Kirk had showered and shaved, and after he'd dressed, he'd rethought the day and what had happened. He questioned his motives and the reasons why he was treating her so harshly. He didn't like the answers he'd been forced to give himself.

He knew she was from a different world than he and was used to certain things foreign to him. Kirk knew he'd been rough with her and knew, too, that it was he who was to blame.

She wasn't disappointing me, he'd told himself, *I'm disappointing me.* With that thought, Kirk realized that he'd been letting Cassandra and her father rule his actions. He resented having to baby-sit a grown woman because of a spoiled whim. He also resented the fact that his emotions were fighting his common sense. He had to think of Cassandra as his ward, not as the woman who, if she were just a little different, he would have desired as no other.

Kirk sensed a loneliness in her that brought out an obligation to help ease her into her new life. He knew all too well what it was like to be alone in the world. The least he could do was not to let her feel totally alienated.

That's why he'd gone to her room and apologized, in his offhanded way, for his treatment of her. *And tonight,* he promised himself, lifting the drink and gazing at his reflection in the bar mirror, *I will act like a gentleman.*

With his mind made up, he put down his drink. Then he saw Cassandra walk into the lounge. He didn't move. For a moment, he just stared into the mirror, his chest strangely tight.

She looked too good to be real. Her dress fit like a glove, and he could see the rise and fall of her full breasts through the material. The narrow yet perfect symmetry of her waist was accented by the clasped belt.

Turning slowly, he gazed directly into her eyes. "Drink?"

Cassandra shook her head, unwilling to take the chance that her voice might fail. She had steeled herself against any reaction to Kirk, but when she saw him, her heart began to race out of control.

"Shall we eat?"

At last she managed a word. "Yes."

Kirk stood and took her elbow in his hand. Cassandra stiffened but forced herself to ignore the tentacles of fire emanating from his touch.

They went into the small dining room and were seated immediately. Cassandra was thankful that the room was decorated in the traditional motel style—bright lights and formica tabletops.

The hostess handed them their menus, and Cassandra looked hers over.

"It's not Le Blanc, but you can trust the steaks."

Her eyes flicked over the top of the menu to see if he was being sarcastic, but he wasn't looking at her. "Thank you," she replied, fighting the tension that once again laid claim to her every action.

A few moments later a smiling waitress appeared, dressed in a cowgirl outfit. "May I take your orders?" she asked sweetly, looking directly at Kirk.

A flare of anger surged at this slight, but Cassandra quickly squelched her feelings when Kirk, ignoring the waitress, looked at her. "Have you made up your mind?" he asked.

Cassandra gave him a full smile. "I think I'll have the New York cut, rare," she stated, looking at the waitress,

whose face was now a beet-red from the unspoken repri-
mand of Kirk's answer.

"And I'll have the same," Kirk stated.

After taking the salad and vegetable orders, the waitress
hurriedly left, and Cassandra was again aware of Kirk's
intense scrutiny. "Thank you," she said.

Kirk nodded his head in a simple gesture. Before they
could start another conversation, the waitress reappeared
with their salads.

Cassandra glanced at Kirk over the rim of her coffee cup.
The meal had been more pleasant than she'd thought
possible. They had talked, but only lightly, never once
delving into a topic that might create tension. By the time
coffee had been served, she was pleasantly relaxed.

"The food was excellent, especially the steak," she
commented after putting her cup down.

"That's what the West is known for," Kirk replied, "but
I'm glad you enjoyed it. Tired?" he asked. "It's been a
long day." Even so, Kirk was used to longer days. At the
ranch, he was up by five and worked late into the eve-
nings.

"Not really; besides, we gained two hours during the
flight."

"There's not a whole lot to do around here at night,
except for a few honky-tonks. Ever been to one?"

"No."

"Want to?"

Warily Cassandra wondered if he was putting her on or
not. She decided not. "I'd love to. I'm not ready for sleep
yet."

Kirk called for the check, signed it, and escorted Cassandra to the rented car. Before she got in, she looked up. Her

breath caught for a moment as the beauty of the western sky spread out in all its glory.

It was a moonless night, but even without the luminescence of the pale globe, the sky was filled with the silver light of countless stars. Not a cloud was in the sky, and the sparkling stars were a calming vision of delight.

"I've never seen a sky like this anywhere in the world," she whispered as she finally got into the car.

They drove in a vastly different silence than the last time they had been in the car. Ten minutes after leaving the motel's restaurant, they entered a small country and western lounge incongruously named the Cow Palace.

The instant Cassandra stepped inside, she felt like a foreigner. Even though she'd taken pains to wear something that was not out of place, she knew she was overdressed in comparison to the other women, who wore jeans or light cotton skirts. Everyone wore cowboy boots; she wore fashionably expensive shoes.

Forcing herself to put on an air of disinterest, Cassandra followed Kirk to a small table, where they sat and ordered drinks.

At the far end of the lounge, a trio, two men and a woman, played instruments and sang mournful love songs. "Why are all country songs so sad?" she asked.

"They reflect life," Kirk responded, his gaze once again intense.

Cassandra tried to relax as much as possible, but whenever she looked at the dance floor, all she could see were people dancing and holding each other close, seeming to be apart from the rest of the world. There was an undercurrent in the lounge, a feeling of suppressed excitement that came close to a sense of belonging, that everyone seemed to share. Everyone except her.

It was a feeling she found herself envying. Shoring up her image of nonchalance, she made her eyes take on a bored, uncaring glaze.

"What do you think?" Kirk asked after studying her obviously well-rehearsed reactions for several long minutes.

"It's different," she admitted honestly.

"Is that bad or good?"

"Neither."

"This, too, is part of ranch life. After working hard all day, and all week, the hands come to places like this, where they can be themselves and enjoy their free time."

"They all seem to have a sort of . . . camaraderie."

"When they're not fighting." Kirk accented his words with a short laugh.

"Do they do that a lot?"

"That depends on what you mean by a lot. Cassandra," he said, his voice changing as he spoke her name. To Cassandra it sounded like more of a caress than a word. "Why are you going to Twin Rivers?"

Cassandra took a deep breath, intuitively sensing that the time for game-playing and immutable facades was over. The tension returned, enveloping them in a shroud of solitude that made her conscious that at this very point in time, something was changing between them. She thought of twenty lies to tell him but discarded each before it was formed. In her heart, as well as in her mind, she knew that only the truth would do.

"I have to. I need to."

"Need to what?" he asked, his voice low, his eyes piercing.

"It's very complicated. . . ."

"So is life, Cassandra, and you've put yourself into my life. You're going to be watching the job I do. All I want to know is why."

Cassandra laughed lightly but did not break eye contact. "My first impulse was to say 'it's none of your business,' but it is. Kirk, I . . ." Cassandra paused to collect her thoughts. "I've spent my life doing absolutely nothing, other than having fun and spending my father's money with a vengeance. I'm twenty-seven years old and I've come to realize that pretty soon I'll have wasted my life, unless I . . ."

Kirk watched her carefully. He had sensed from the moment she first started speaking, that her words were coming from the heart. When she stopped to look at him with her large eyes, he'd seen her waiting for him to respond. Instead he waited silently.

"You don't make things very easy," she said, lowering her voice as the music ended.

"All I asked was a simple question."

"But the answer's complicated. I have to prove to myself that I can do something useful with my life." She didn't know why it was so important for Kirk to understand what she was saying, it just was.

"So you went to your father and asked him to give you Twin Rivers?"

"Not exactly. . . .I asked him to give me a chance to change my life, to prove that I could be good in business. Twin Rivers was his idea."

"It doesn't seem a logical choice to me," Kirk commented lightly, but his eyes were anything but light.

"Oh, it was very logical," Cassandra stated in bitter, hushed tones.

Kirk waited patiently for her to continue, but she didn't. It was as if a curtain had fallen across her eyes and did not reopen for several seconds.

Cassandra tried to rid her mind of the old fear her words had evoked. There were two parts to her father's plan. The first she couldn't tell Kirk about. The other she could.

"If I . . . we don't make a profit this year, then I'll have to end my short-lived career and fulfill the bargain I made with my father. If Twin Rivers doesn't go into the black, I'll have to do something I don't want to."

"Then I guess we'll have to work together to make the ranch profitable. But it won't be easy," Kirk said, momentarily lowering his defenses in the face of her own confession and, at the same time, wondering about Gregory Leeds' words to him about Cassandra.

Cassandra heard him but could not believe he was actually saying the words. Yet the look on his face was enough to lend belief.

"I . . . I'll need your help, Kirk," she admitted aloud for the first time.

Kirk tensed. Her unexpected plea had struck him hard. He wanted to reach out and hold her. "I'm willing to try," he said instead.

"Thank you. But, as you said, it won't be easy."

"It won't be that hard."

"It has to be. You see, Father wouldn't take a chance on losing. He always wins, and he doesn't want me to succeed."

Kirk's brow furrowed. "What do you mean?"

"Father doesn't think I have a chance to make the ranch show a profit."

"How can you be so certain?" Kirk asked, his voice sharp as he sat straighter.

Cassandra wouldn't tell him the main reason—her fear—but she had sensed when she'd gone over the books that something wasn't right about Twin Rivers' losses. Too many of them had seemed unnecessary, even in her inexperienced judgment.

"He seemed so confident that I wouldn't be able to make the ranch profitable, as if there were some sort of a fail-safe means to stop profits," she reiterated. Then she took yet another deep breath and smiled at Kirk. "You never asked me about the man in the lobby."

"It was none of my business," Kirk replied, only half truthfully. He had wanted to know, but he would never ask; that wasn't his way.

"His name is Somner Barwell. He's rich and considered to be one of the world's most eligible bachelors. He's part of this, too. Kirk, if I fail, I lose more than just a career; I lose my life. The bargain I made with my father was that if Twin Rivers stays in the red, I have to marry Somner."

It took Kirk a few seconds for the full impact of her words to register. It took another moment for him to speak. "This isn't the eighteen-hundreds. Marriages aren't arranged anymore. He can't force you to marry anyone, no matter what he says."

"My father is a very powerful man. So is Somner Barwell's father. They want this marriage. Kirk, men like my father are the new royalty of the world. Marriages between these 'royal' families happen all the time. It promotes business and lessens competition."

"What about you? Doesn't he care about you? Besides, you're not a possession, you have a mind of your own," Kirk stated, angry at the machinations of the upper echelons of the business world.

Cassandra couldn't help the surge of pleasure his words

gave her. "He cared about me once, but now I think he cares more about his companies. Still, I made a promise. I *never* break my promises," Cassandra whispered. "I have to go through with this. Especially after yesterday. Kirk, I never knew Somner was like that. He frightened me; he was like a stranger."

Kirk studied her face intently. "I guess that means we have no choice but to make a profit."

"If we can," Cassandra restated, not letting her happiness at his agreement shadow reality. "But I still think Father has an ace in the hole that he hopes will let him win."

"So do I," Kirk said suddenly. "But doesn't that make this deal of yours invalid if he knows you can't possibly turn a profit?"

Cassandra shook her head. There might be something hidden, but she was sure that her father was counting on her fear of horses more than anything else. "My father can be devious, and he's a hard businessman. But he's never lied to me. Even if the deck is stacked in his favor, there'll be a way to win. We just have to find it."

"You could always run away, start a new life somewhere," he suggested. Yet as he spoke he found himself hoping that she would not take him seriously.

"I can't run away from myself," she stated. Once again Kirk saw a break in her facade; saw a hint of determination. Kirk found himself wanting to believe her; but he wasn't any more sure of Gregory Leeds than he was of his daughter.

Making himself try to see the truth lurking within her hazel-green eyes, Kirk knew that he would do his best to find a way to win. But, he admitted to himself, it was chancy, at best. "Do you love him?" he asked in a husky voice.

"Somner?" Cassandra asked. "No. At one time there was something but not anymore. Especially after yesterday."

In the silence that followed her reply, Kirk could not help thinking just how complicated Cassandra Leeds had suddenly shown herself to be. Surprisingly he found himself happy with that. The only dark shadow in his mind was caused by a combination of Gregory Leeds and Somner Barwell.

The lights of the lounge flickered twice, and the trio's singer spoke into the microphone. "Last call, cowboys. Last dance, too," she said as the trio began to play a slow, melodious love song.

"I didn't realize how late it was," Cassandra said without taking her gaze from him.

"Dance?" he asked.

"I thought you'd never ask," she replied, saying the very thing she knew she shouldn't.

Kirk led her to the dance floor, conscious of the many eyes following them, but uncaring at the same time. He didn't know why he'd asked her to dance; in fact, he was more than positive he shouldn't have. However, seeing her in the low light of the lounge, her moist lips looking soft and pliant, had made him ask her.

On the dance floor, he took her in his arms and held her gently. Through the few short inches that separated them, he felt the heat of her body as if he wore no clothes.

Cassandra followed his lead, bending gracefully with his movements, luxuriating within the strength of his arms, and never once wondering why she was there.

The music, so different from what she was used to, only accented the dissemblance of her own perceptions. She gazed deeply into his eyes, allowing herself to be drawn within them. This time, when his hand had grasped hers, and his other hand had gone around her waist, no leaping flames had scorched her body; only a gentle warmth ebbed and flowed within her.

But when Kirk turned them gracefully on the dance floor, another couple bumped into them, pushing Cassandra into Kirk's muscular chest. She gasped when she was pressed to his powerful torso, thankful for the excuse of another for her reaction.

"Are you all right?"

Cassandra couldn't speak. She just nodded. But, as Kirk looked down at her from his incredible height, she did not pull away. Instead she let herself flow with the music and the wonderful sensations invading her body and mind. It was as if she had been transported in time to another place, another world. It was a mystical moment, a rare instance of peace, given to her when there should only have been doubt, confusion, and fear.

Every second that passed in Kirk's strong arms was like magic, but, like magic, she knew the illusion would disappear the moment the music ended. Reality would have to become, once again, the rule of the night.

Kirk's arms had tightened reflexively around her, while his eyes swept across her face. When he was sure that she was all right, he reluctantly loosened his hold, trying his best to ignore the fiery sensations her softly curved body was generating upon his.

When she did not pull back, Kirk was not sorry. He bent his head and caught the clinging scent of her perfume, mixed within the clean freshness of her hair.

Suddenly Kirk found himself in a battle with his emotions, fighting hard to hold back from kissing her the way his senses demanded.

He moved with the music, guiding Cassandra's subtly swaying body, caring not what the future might bring, content only for the present. Kirk knew that with their arrival at the ranch, their already changing roles must once again change.

She is the boss's daughter, he reminded himself again.

When the music ended, Cassandra reluctantly stepped back. "Thank you," she whispered.

"Thank you," Kirk replied. Silently, for neither of them was willing to break the soft mood enveloping them, they left the Cow Palace and returned to the motel. At their doors, they faced each other, and Cassandra felt the tension build around them like a volcano about to erupt.

"I had a lovely time tonight. Thank you, Kirk." He gazed steadily at her until she thought she would scream. Her eyes continually swept the planes of his face, drinking in his rugged good looks. She saw his eyes doing the same, and for a fleeting and hopeful second, she thought he would kiss her.

But he didn't kiss her. Instead Kirk stepped back. "You're welcome, Cassandra. I'll leave a wake-up call for eight. After breakfast, we'll fly home."

Cassandra nodded, hiding her disappointment, yet not certain that she had really wanted him to kiss her. The most curious thing of all, she thought as she opened her door, was the way he'd said home had tugged strangely at her heart.

An hour later Kirk was still unable to sleep. He sat in a club chair by the window, looking out into the night. His mind was a rolling symphony of discordant thoughts as he tried to settle his emotions and the startling reactions that had risen during the evening with Cassandra.

He remembered the few moments before she'd gone into her room. He had wanted to take her in his arms, press her tightly to him, and kiss her inviting lips. But he hadn't. Instead he'd tightened an iron will of control on his emotions.

When she'd spoken about her ''deal'' with her father, Kirk had almost lost his temper, but held himself back when he'd realized once again that Cassandra and Gregory Leeds lived in a different world. But Kirk had not been able to help wondering just what kind of game Gregory Leeds was playing.

Apparently Cassandra Leeds had no idea that her father had told Kirk that she was to be only a figurehead. But, Kirk realized, Cassandra had every intention of trying to run Twin Rivers.

That was not his only concern. The man he had stopped from manhandling her was another. He had heard the ugly tone of Somner Barwell's voice and had seen the hard, dangerous glint in the man's eyes when he'd forced Barwell's hands from Cassandra.

He didn't want that man to possess Cassandra Leeds no matter what. *Why?* he asked himself. Kirk knew the answer but refused to hear it. *She's not for him* is what he tried to make himself believe.

In that moment, Kirk promised himself that he would help her if she really meant what she'd said to him. That was the only thing that bothered him now. Was she determined to do what she said, or was it just a rich person's game that she was seducing him into?

Chapter Seven

$\mathcal{B}$ecause of severe thunderstorms over the Rockies they did not leave Wyoming as early as planned. After sitting in the airport's small pilots' lounge for three hours, they were finally cleared for takeoff. The mood of last night still clung to them, yet each was wary of saying too much.

The flight was a smooth one and Cassandra, still somewhat tired from the very long day, fell asleep. Kirk let her sleep, happy for the time he had to organize his thoughts before reaching the ranch.

For Kirk, the evening had been a revelation of sorts. He'd gotten several glimpses of the Cassandra Leeds behind the mask. Just before he fell asleep, he discovered that he liked *that* Cassandra Leeds very much.

He wondered if the mask, and everything that went with it, would return when they were at the ranch. Then he refused to ask himself that kind of question. He knew he would just have to wait and see how Cassandra Leeds would prove herself.

As he flew the plane he occasionally glanced at Cassandra's peacefully sleeping face, studying it intently until every line and feature was etched indelibly in his mind.

Kirk was flying above the clouds, but when he neared the ranch, he descended in a slow, steady line. Breaking through the clouds, he smiled at the familiar terrain below.

"Cassandra," he called in a gentle voice.

Cassandra heard her name called from a great distance and struggled from sleep to reality. Opening her eyes, she glanced at Kirk.

"Have a good sleep?" he asked.

"Sorry," she said as she sat straighter. "I didn't mean to doze off."

"Flying in clouds is boring; you did the right thing," he told her. "We're here."

"Here?" Cassandra asked, stretching her cramped muscles.

"Twin Rivers."

Cassandra looked down and her breath caught. Beneath her, extending for miles, were rolling hills and deep valleys. There were mountains in every direction she looked. At first glance, they appeared to be harsh and barren, but their reddish-brown color was striking and bold.

"Beautiful," she whispered.

"It is," Kirk agreed. "Look to your right."

There she saw a more level area than what had been below her moments before. She studied the terrain, trying to see what Kirk wanted her to. A minute later she saw thousands of dark dots.

"That's one of our herds," he said.

"So many," she whispered as she tried to find the edge of the herd.

"Not really; they're spread out. About twenty-thousand head."

"That's a lot."

"Not enough. Beef prices are still down. Hopefully they'll go up soon. The market trend seems to be pointing that way. But," he said, pausing to look at her, "we'll talk business tomorrow. Right now is your first tour of the ranch."

Kirk banked the plane and the herd of cattle disappeared. Ten minutes later he was flying over a two-lane road. "This is the western border of the property. It extends for eleven miles."

Cassandra watched silently and began to understand just how large a hundred-and-twenty-thousand acres of ranch was. They were flying no more than five-hundred feet above the ground, and Cassandra could see everything.

"Look to your right," Kirk said. When Cassandra turned, he continued to speak. "The main house is the one with the red-tile roof—Spanish tile—the ranch's offices are on the main level. On the second floor are bedroom suites for visiting businessmen, or Leeds Corporation people. You'll be living in one of them."

Cassandra was impressed by the size of the house, and by the sprawling layout of all the buildings. Twin Rivers was a far cry from the ranch in Wyoming. Off to one side of the house was a road that ran for as far as she could see. It seemed to be a dividing line of some sort. To the right was the main house and, separated from it by a large lawn, was a smaller house with the same Spanish-tiled roof. A little farther on was yet another small house. Behind those structures, at a good distance, were four long narrow buildings.

From one of the long buildings, a trail of smoke rose into the air, dissipating a hundred feet up. Kirk flew over the buildings, banked the plane, and circled.

"The second house is where I live. The buildings behind it are the bunkhouses and the dining hall. The staff is getting supper ready now."

Farther away was a blacktop landing strip, complete with two gas pumps. Finishing the circle, Kirk straightened the plane and flew across the dividing road. Beneath them, Cassandra saw a whole new set of buildings. Several barns, a huge silo, and three long stables were the first. Then she saw the corrals, and the horses within them.

"The stables hold a hundred and fifteen horses; all the workhorses for the ranch. Over there," he said, pointing to another series of buildings, "are the breeding pens."

Cassandra had determined the moment she'd boarded the plane to keep her emotions in check. Although the fear rose with every reference to horses, she did not let it show on her rigid features. Yet she could not talk, either.

For the next twenty-five minutes, Cassandra sat quietly while Kirk gave her a bird's-eye view of where she would be living and working for the next twelve months.

By the end of the tour, Cassandra's fear had vanished, replaced by a sense of awed beauty. As they flew, the clouds that had been with them since Wyoming finally dissolved, and the jewellike blueness of the Arizona sky had appeared. The sun, near the edge of the horizon, glowed warmly, lighting everything with soft shades of pale gold, and Cassandra fell in love with the land beneath her.

They passed over a second herd, which was as large as

the first, and then Kirk flew toward a hilly ridge that she soon discovered was the edge of a narrow valley. In the valley was a sight that held her in thrall for several long seconds, until again, Cassandra forced herself to control her fears. Beneath them, roaming freely, was the herd of Appaloosa horses. After her initial shock at seeing them, Cassandra relaxed a bit. It wasn't too bad from the air, she told herself.

At the northern edge of the property, Kirk banked the plane in a lazy downward spiral, coming within a hundred feet of the foothills. "There's a special place I want you to see. Watch carefully; it's coming up now."

Cassandra held her breath as they skimmed the hilltops. Then her exhale sounded loudly within the cabin. Without warning, a magnificent waterfall appeared before her eyes. It was a narrow band of water, cascading from a few feet below a jagged cliff, and spraying outward in a foaming array of colors that struck several rocky ledges before reaching the pool at its base.

"It's not much of a tourist attraction, but it's ours," Kirk said.

"It's . . ." Cassandra began, searching for the right word, "perfect," she said at last.

"Yes, it is."

On the way back to the airstrip, Kirk flew over several plowed fields. "We try to grow as much feed of our own as possible. It helps save money."

Before they landed, Kirk had taken a little side trip and flown closer to Phoenix to show Cassandra the outskirts of the city.

After that, with dusk growing thick in the air, they returned to the ranch. Just before they landed, Kirk spoke again. "I think it would be a good idea for you to acclimate yourself to the ranch. For the next few days, I'll take you around and show you every part of the operation."

"That sounds good," she said.

"After you're familiar with the workings of the ranch, we can sit down and find a way to make more money with what we have. All right?" he asked, his gaze flickering between her face and the upcoming landing strip.

"Fine," she said. Things were going much better than she'd thought possible, following the terrible beginning with Kirk. Also, Cassandra realized as Kirk landed the plane smoothly, there had not been one moment of tension, anger, or sarcasm throughout the entire day.

They unloaded Cassandra's five suitcases and piled them into a Land-Rover with the Twin Rivers logo on its doors, and Kirk started to drive toward the buildings. He did not go to the main house however, but went instead to the dining hall, which was empty except for the cook.

"Lucy, this is Miss Cassandra Leeds. She'll be staying with us for a while."

"Pleased to meet ya," Lucy replied with a smile and a nod.

"Lucy is the person who keeps us going," Kirk said in a soft voice. "She's the ranch's cook, and the best in Arizona."

"He says that because he's afraid I'll ask for a raise," Lucy stated, yet her smile of pleasure negated her words.

"Lucy, we're starving," Kirk admitted.

Even as he spoke, Cassandra felt and heard her stomach rumble at the mention of food, and the gurgling sound reached the others' ears. Cassandra turned red. "I think ya'll made your point," Lucy said jokingly. "Sit while I get you some supper."

Five minutes later Lucy brought two plates heaped with food and placed them before Kirk and Cassandra. Cassandra looked at her plate, her eyes questioning its contents.

"Stew," Kirk said as he picked up his fork and began to eat. Tentatively Cassandra lifted up a small piece of meat and tasted it. She was pleasantly surprised at the rich taste of the stew.

"It don't look like much, but your stomach doesn't have eyes," Lucy commented sagely as she set down a tray with coffee cups on it.

After giving Kirk and Cassandra their coffee, she stepped back. "I best get back to work. Nice meeting you, Miss Cassandra."

"She seems nice," Cassandra commented after Lucy went into the kitchen.

"As long as you stay on her good side. Otherwise . . ." he said with a patently false smile of warning.

"She's a good cook."

"As I said, the best in Arizona."

They finished their meal in a warm silence, and afterward Kirk drove Cassandra to the main house and brought her up to her suite.

At the door, Kirk looked into Cassandra's eyes. She gazed up at him, her heart beating fast as she drank in his handsome face.

"If you'd like," Kirk said a moment later, "you can join us in the dining hall for breakfast. We eat at five, and the men are out and working by six."

"Five. . . . The sun's not even up that early," she joked, but saw no humorous response in Kirk's well-chiseled features.

"If you prefer eating alone, your kitchen has been well

stocked. Either way, we'll start your tour of Twin Rivers tomorrow at six.''

"I never have more than coffee in the morning. I'll be ready," Cassandra promised.

From the time Kirk had helped bring her luggage up until he left, Cassandra had paid no real attention to her new home. But with Kirk's footsteps echoing on the stairs, Cassandra turned and looked around.

The suite was almost spartan in its decoration, yet it had a homey flavor that made her feel very comfortable. The suite consisted of a living room, bedroom, study, bath and kitchen, all decorated in a style she could only describe as "western conservative." Thick wood beams ran along the ceiling and Oriental carpets in each room added a touch of authority to the wood and leather furniture.

When she finished her inspection, Cassandra quickly and efficiently put all her possessions away and, stifling a yawn, took a long, relaxing shower, after which she went into her new bedroom and got ready for sleep.

Yawning again, Cassandra realized how tired she was. "Country air," she told herself as she lay down and fell into a deep dreamless sleep.

Cassandra finished tying her sneakers and stood. She walked to the window and peered out into the early dawn. The sun had not yet risen in the gray-blue sky.

Cassandra adjusted the top to her rust-colored jogging suit and went into the kitchen to check on the automatic coffee maker she'd started before dressing.

The aroma of coffee greeted her when she stepped into the sunny kitchen set in one corner of the suite, complete with gas oven, range, and a nice-size refrigerator, which was separated from the range by a counter with a stainless-steel sink. The two café-curtained windows made the room seem larger than it really was.

In the center of the kitchen was a butcher block table with four ladder-back chairs. A telephone extension was on the wall behind the table, and the white tile floor added more brightness to the room.

Cassandra poured a cup of coffee and sat down at the table. She tried to concentrate on preparing herself for her first day of work but found her mind wandering. Not even the sounds of the ranch coming to life were able to pull her from her thoughts.

Finishing her coffee, Cassandra realized that today marked the second day of her future, and the beginning of her test. "I will not fail," she whispered, repeating the litany that had become so much a part of her.

She glanced at her watch. Five forty-five. Fifteen minutes until she was to meet Kirk and begin her first day of work. Cassandra rose and poured herself another cup of coffee. As she did she looked out the window.

She saw the ranch hands leaving the dining hall. They all looked alike, dressed in jeans and light cotton shirts. They all wore boots, and several of the men wore riding chaps. All of them wore cowboy hats.

But one in particular caught Cassandra's attention. It was the ranch hand's walk. It was different. The ranch hand was shorter, too. A moment later the cowboy took off his hat, and Cassandra's cup wavered at her mouth. The ranch hand wasn't a cowboy—the person was a woman.

The moment she'd taken her hat off, Cassandra saw a thick bounty of shoulder-length red hair sparkle in the morning sun.

"Well, I'll be. . . ."

Kirk had never mentioned that a woman worked as a ranch hand.

There were a lot of things Kirk had not mentioned, Cassandra thought as she placed her cup in the sink and started out. She was not about to be late on her first day. Kirk would be waiting for her in front of the house.

Passing a mirror, Cassandra stopped to check herself over. The jogging suit was comfortable and casual, and her sneakers matched it well. Her long hair was pulled back and clipped at the crown of her head, where she hoped it would stay for the rest of the day.

Satisfied that she was dressed reasonably well for a ranch, Cassandra left the apartment and walked through the still-empty house. The office staff would not be in until eight, Kirk had told her.

Stepping out into the early morning sunlight, Cassandra looked around for Kirk. She found him standing ten feet away. "Good morning," she called, feeling a pleasant warmth at the sight of his tall, strong body, encased within a pair of snug-fitting jeans that accented the leanness of his abdomen and outlined his muscular thighs. His shirt, a light denim, showed off the wide breadth of his chest.

"Hopefully," Kirk responded as he looked her over. He took a deep breath and exhaled sharply. "We're going on a ground tour of the ranch, you know."

"Of course I know. I'm not senile."

Kirk tried to keep the exasperation he felt out of his voice. "Cassandra, this is a ranch, not a resort. I think you should put on a pair of boots."

"Boots?" she asked, puzzled by his request. "Why?"

"You can manage in that fancy running suit, but your ankles are going to get very sore if you wear sneakers," he explained tolerantly, trying to maintain a high level of patience.

"Why should sneakers make me sore?"

"Because there's no protection. The stirrups will rub your skin raw without boots."

"Stirrups?" she whispered, his words striking her with the force of a tornado. Within her tight stomach, the old familiar twisting, sickening sensations began.

"Yes, stirrups. They're part of the saddle. They help you stay on your horse," he said, unable to keep the sarcasm out of his voice. "I told you we're going to see the ranch from the ground today. Our horses are saddled and ready."

Cassandra tried to speak but failed. The coffee that had felt so warm and good only a few minutes before, was rapidly turning sour in her stomach. Her neck tightened, and she could feel the beginning of a tension-induced headache. She had to find a way out. She had to!

Looking around, Cassandra saw the same vehicle Kirk had driven to the ranch in, a Land-Rover. Summoning up her resolve, Cassandra finally spoke. "Horses," she said, shaking her head. "I would just as soon be comfortable." Fear made her voice sound imperious. "We'll take that," she stated, pointing to the vehicle.

Kirk stared at her, at the strange tightness of her features, even as he fought to hold back his anger. But as she spoke in her distant and arrogant manner, Kirk felt his understanding of her diminish, the understanding he had so carefully cultivated over the past thirty-six hours.

He made himself hold back his first angry retort and even kept up his now forced smile. "Of course," he said through clenched teeth, "we wouldn't want you to get dirty."

With that, Kirk turned and strode stiffly to the jeep. Cassandra wanted to call out, to explain what had hap-

pened, but she couldn't. If she did, he would see how
frightened she was. She couldn't let him.

Pretending not to be bothered by his words, Cassandra
walked to the Land-Rover, opened the door, and got in.
Before she was fully seated, Kirk had pressed down the
accelerator, and dirt and gravel spewed from beneath the
rear wheels. Cassandra said nothing as she was thrown
rudely and forcefully against the seat back.

Here we go again, she told herself.

For Cassandra, the next four days passed in a whirlwind
of activity and hostility as she continued to insist that Kirk
use the Land-Rover to show her the ranch.

And from that first morning, when she'd refused to ride
the horses, Kirk had once again changed. He didn't revert
to the angry, acerbic man she'd first met, but he was a far
cry from the warm and friendly companion of that wonderful night in Wyoming.

What he had become was a distant, standoffish person
who replied to all her questions succinctly, never volunteer-
ing a word more than was necessary.

He used no sarcasm; he offered no extra help. That he
tolerated her was obvious; that he disliked her was a
concrete fact, brought home with every glance of his steely,
chiseled, and immobile features.

Yet not once, as he indoctrinated her into the workings of
the ranch, did he ever lose his patience. His voice was
always calm, his manner cool and efficient. During every
minute Cassandra spent with him, she felt the distance
between them grow. At times she wanted to scream, to yell
that she was only human. But she only made herself act just
the way he did—cool and detached. Cassandra knew she

was using this front as a defense, but she also knew she had no choice.

By the third day, Cassandra acknowledged that every article of clothing she'd brought was useless. So she had driven into town and gone shopping at a western clothing store, where she bought everything she would need, from boots to hats. She'd spent a small fortune, but that didn't matter. Although her father had cut off her credit cards, she had her own bank account and the first week's salary from work to draw on.

When she'd returned to the ranch, she took all the packages upstairs and put the clothing away. She now owned a wardrobe that was appropriate. The next morning, she'd seen the briefest flicker of animation in Kirk's face when she'd shown up in jeans, a plaid shirt, and her new boots.

But he hadn't said a word. At noon, after they'd returned from the north range where Kirk had shown Cassandra the fencework being done, he suggested she change out of the boots.

"Why?"

"New boots have to be broken in. After a couple of hours, you'll start getting blisters."

Accepting his advice, Cassandra changed into her sneakers for the rest of the day. Her feet were fine, and she had been grateful for his suggestion. But when they'd returned to the main house and she'd thanked him, all he'd done was nod his head.

By the end of the day, when he'd dropped her off at the main house, the tension was thick between them. Before she could walk to the house, Kirk spoke.

"I've called a meeting for eight o'clock," he told her.

"For what?"

"For you to formally be introduced to your ranch hands."

"Where?"

"The dining hall."

"I'll be there at eight." With that, Cassandra turned her back on him and went into the house.

Cassandra had eaten a light supper alone, as she had done every night since her arrival at Twin Rivers, and was trying to relax before going to the meeting.

She knew that she faced a test with the ranch hands, and braced herself for the meeting.

She had already noticed, from time to time, when Kirk had driven her past the employees, the way their eyes had followed her.

The phone's ring shattered her thoughts and, reaching out, she picked up the receiver. "Yes?"

"Good evening, Cassie."

Cassandra tensed. "Hello, Father."

"How are things?"

I haven't run away, she wanted to say. "Everything is going well," she replied instead.

"I'm glad to hear that. You know I worry about you," Gregory Leeds stated.

Cassandra's lips, drawn as tightly as a bowstring, showed her anger plainly. Yet her father, thousands of miles away, could not see them.

"Do you, Father? Or are you worrying about the Barwell merger?"

"That's unkind, Cassie. I only called to see if you were settled in."

"You said you required monthly progress reports. It's

only been three days. I'll call you in twenty-seven days, Father.''

"Cassandra, if I told you that I wished you luck, would you accept that?"

Cassandra remembered the many times when she had been growing up, that she'd heard her father talking with his executives. "Make your opposition trust you. Weaken them, not with flattery, but with openness. Make them believe you are sympathetic to them, but remember, when you deal with others, they're your enemy. Think of them that way. Always protect yourself." That was one of Gregory Leeds' philosophies, and Cassandra knew better than to trust him.

"Cassandra?" her father asked after the long silence.

"No, Father, I can't accept that. I'm your daughter; I know you."

"No, Cassie, you used to know me. Very well, I'll speak to you in twenty-seven days. Good night," he said.

Cassandra, her eyes blurring, hung up the phone without another word. She shouldn't have said that to him, she knew, but she hadn't been able to stop the words. She should have played along with him, let him believe she was just a lonely, spoiled little girl, but she couldn't. Not anymore.

Her father's phone call disturbed her greatly. She could hear the gloating in his voice and knew he was waiting for her to throw in the towel. "Give up!" was what his tone said even as he had wished her luck.

Standing, Cassandra began to pace within the confines of the room. So much was happening to her all at once, and she was having a harder and harder time coping.

For too many years, Cassandra had run away from her troubles and problems. She had been running since she was nine. *Running from what?* she asked herself. *From fear?* She knew it wasn't just fear, but what it was she didn't know.

I used to be so happy, she thought, gazing at her new surroundings. It was true, at least until the accident. That was when her life had really changed. The fear that had come from the accident was part of it, but there was more. She had lost her will to do things and had become satisfied with whatever was easiest.

School had been a joke. She had breezed through the prestigious private school and through college without really trying. She had a quick memory that saved her many long hours of study.

After dropping out of college, she had found herself listlessly wandering around the world, caught up in the frenetic pace of her wealthy friends. Her father denied her nothing, and gave her whatever she asked for, except for the things she really needed, the things that money couldn't buy.

But here at Twin Rivers she found herself unprepared for reality. She had thought it would be easy to take over a company and prove herself to her father. After all, she was not only a quick study, but she was Gregory Leeds' daughter.

Only it wasn't working out that way. The people who surrounded her now didn't know her and acted as if she did not belong here, although her father owned the ranch and paid their salaries.

At last, Cassandra stopped pacing as a new thought intruded into her troubled mind. *Not only do I have to prove myself to my father, but I have to prove myself to them, too,* she realized. *It's not fair!*

Suddenly aware that it was time to leave, Cassandra

calmed her troubled thoughts as she went to the mirror to check her clothing one last time. She was more than satisfied with her appearance. She wore a pair of tan denims with a yellow checked shirt tucked neatly into the waistband. She had her boots on, which raised her height another two inches. Her dark hair was pulled back severely, accenting the smooth angles of her lightly made-up face.

Then she willed her walls of defense to stay strong before she turned and left the apartment to face the inevitable. When she reached the dining hall, she saw it was already filled with ranch hands.

The moment she entered, every eye turned in her direction. Ignoring the stares, Cassandra kept her head straight and proud and walked to where Kirk stood. When she reached him and sat in the chair next to his, Kirk rose and the room fell silent.

Conscious that all the hands were now staring openly at her, Cassandra looked up at Kirk. She wished she hadn't, because she saw a shadowy smile on his full lips that told her he was enjoying himself tonight.

The moment he spoke, she knew the truth of her observation. Without ceremony, he introduced her.

"Listen up," Kirk called in a loud voice. The hands turned their attention from Cassandra to Kirk. "As most of you know, there's a new face on the ranch." Kirk paused and glanced down at Cassandra before he continued. His eyes bored into hers.

"Miss Cassandra Leeds is a vice president of Leeds International and is now in charge of the Twin Rivers Corporation. Miss Leeds," he said as he abruptly finished and sat down.

Cassandra rose, moistening her lips as she did, and looked out at what seemed to be an endless sea of unfriendly faces. In that instant, when she saw their expressions, she knew they thought her to be the company's watchdog.

She spoke quickly, although she had nothing to say, and her voice was tinged with the same protective imperiousness she had used toward Kirk since her arrival.

"I hope that I will soon get to meet each of you individually. If you have any questions, please do not hesitate to come to me." As she spoke, she saw the look of disdain on many of their faces. Then she tried to single out one friendly face, and settled on making eye contact with the female ranch hand, whose name she had learned was Jane Paulson. But although there was no disdain on her face, her eyes were as unfriendly as the rest.

After her short speech, she sat down and waited until the meeting ended and everyone except Kirk was gone.

"That was a nasty thing to do," she snapped.

"Nasty? I just introduced you to your employees."

"It was the way you did it."

"That's my way, Miss Leeds," he said, his eyes looking straight through her.

"I told you once that you won't scare me off. Don't try so hard," she advised him in an icy whisper.

"All I want to do, Miss Leeds, is my job—"

"Then do it!" she snapped angrily.

"And," he continued in a level voice, "I think I've spent enough time familiarizing you with the operation."

"Yes, you have," Cassandra replied stiffly.

"Thank you. If you need me tomorrow, I'll be at the corral. We've got horses to break."

Cassandra stared at him for a moment. "I thought there weren't any horses to sell this year."

''We lost a lot, but we still have about thirty head. Good night, Miss Leeds,'' he said as he stood and started out.

''We aren't enemies, Kirk,'' Cassandra shouted before he reached the door.

Kirk turned, his taut face shadowed by the uneven light at the doorway. ''We aren't friends, either,'' he replied in a very low voice as he turned and walked out.

''What are we?'' Cassandra asked the closed door, trying to understand what was making Kirk act the way he was.

Chapter Eight

$\mathcal{K}$irk sat on the high-backed chair, his eyes half closed, the rise and fall of his chest barely visible. It was late, almost midnight, but he couldn't sleep. Too many unanswered questions plagued him. Too many unsolvable problems haunted him when they shouldn't.

Who was Cassandra Leeds? Why did she affect him so strongly? Why did he care what she thought, felt, or even did with her life?

But he did care, and that was his problem. There was another problem, too—the Leeds Corporation. Why were they so complacent with their losses? Why did they reward people who lost money for them? There had to be a reason, and Kirk wanted to know exactly what it was. He had invested too much time, effort, and care in Twin Rivers to have it yanked away from him by the random whims of corporate executives.

Through his narrowed eyes, Kirk saw the light in

Cassandra's bedroom go out. Except for the times he had driven her around the ranch, she had avoided any contact with him. She had even avoided coming into his office when she'd had a question about paperwork; instead she'd used the intercom.

"You won't scare me off," she'd told him earlier. It was the second time she'd used that particular phrase. Was there something she was afraid of? Kirk wondered. Something he couldn't see?

Kirk thought about that special night in Wyoming when he'd sensed her loneliness and frustration. Had he been wrong about her then also? Was she just playing a game with him, making a fool of him? Or had she told him the truth about the bargain she'd made with her father?

"You awake or asleep, boss man?" came a husky, feminine voice.

Kirk opened his eyes and focused on Jane Paulson. "Can't sleep?"

"I've got a lot on my mind," Jane replied as she sat on a chair next to Kirk's.

"You haven't been having any more problems with the men, have you?"

"No, that stopped about three months ago when I realized you were right. They didn't hate me; they just wanted to see if I could hack it."

"Confidence in your own abilities is the proper phrase."

"I try to think in monosyllables these days," she replied with a smile.

"You aren't the only cowboy with a degree," Kirk told her.

"How many others do you know with a degree in clinical psychology?"

"Only a few dozen," Kirk said with a straight face.

"Kirk, what's going on?" Jane asked, her voice serious and piercing.

"With what?"

"With Cassandra Leeds. Why is she here?"

"Twin Rivers is a subsidiary of—"

"Kirk, it's me, your little cousin. Remember?"

Kirk nodded and looked away from Jane for a moment. She was his cousin, and the only blood relative he had. She was nine years his junior, twenty-five.

Jane's mother and his were sisters. She had grown up on the same ranch as Kirk, and although she had tried to fight it, she had learned that ranching was what she really wanted to do with her life.

Six months ago Jane had come to him and asked for a job. He had argued with her, fought against her, but finally gave in, knowing that in his heart, he was proud of her for being honest with herself, facing up to the truth, and taking responsibility for her future.

"I was wrong. I thought I wanted to get away from ranching and from the people in it. That's why I went in for psychology. But it isn't working; I don't like the life on 'the outside.' The people aren't real," she'd said.

"Kirk, Cassandra Leeds?" Jane asked again.

"I don't know. I think her father wants me to baby-sit. She doesn't think so."

"Why are you so hard on her?"

"Hard? I'm just doing my job."

"Why are you lying to yourself?"

"Why are you trying to shrink me?"

"I'm worried about you," she said, her eyes reflecting the truth of her words. "You pretty much raised me. I know you, Kirk. Cassandra Leeds has gotten to you and you don't want to admit it."

It took several moments for Kirk to reply. When he did, his voice was distant. "Cassandra Leeds is a beautiful shell covering a spoiled, shallow, callous excuse for a woman."

"Kirk—"

"Good night, Jane," Kirk whispered as he turned away.

Jane stood silently and walked away; but in her mind were the unspoken words that were a parody of a popular song. *You've got it bad, big cousin. And I don't know if that ain't good!*

Cassandra stopped at the side of the road. She stood there for several long minutes, oblivious of the heat of the day or the dryness in her mouth.

She had spent a long and sleepless night, trying her best to reconcile her actions with reality. She wanted to move forward, to patch up the discordant notes between her and Kirk, and find a way to make Twin Rivers become profitable.

She had discovered that she could not do that by hiding away. She had to go out and see what was happening, learn about more than just the bottom line.

That was why she was standing under the strong Arizona sun, wearing her not yet broken-in boots, and trying to quell the fear-induced rapid beating of her heart. She was about to observe the livestock.

She knew she had to show her face and show Kirk that she wasn't afraid of getting dirty. Taking a deep preparatory breath, Cassandra crossed the road and moved toward the corral, which was ringed with gleefully calling cowboys.

Twenty feet away Cassandra froze. She saw a wild horse jumping in the corral; on its back was Kirk North. The spotted horse looked like a fearsome vision born of a nightmare, and for just a second, she thought she would never see Kirk again.

But the madly bucking horse soon slowed its frantic maneuverings, and Kirk rode him to the side, where another ranch hand took the reins and led him away. When she was able to breathe again, Cassandra edged closer to the corral.

No one seemed to take notice of her; all eyes were on the action within the wood-fenced circle. Once again Cassandra's breath caught as she recognized the only female ranch hand sitting astride one of the unbroken horses.

With the nod of Jane Paulson's head, the man holding the horse released it and Jane was tossed up and down.

Cassandra gripped the wood of the corral so tightly that her knuckles turned white. Her eyes were locked on the battle, and her heart beat wildly with fear for the woman.

Yet Jane seemed unafraid, and Cassandra saw a smile on the woman's face, mixed with determination. For three more minutes she watched Jane rise and fall on the beast's back, until the wild horse began to spin in circles, bucking hard as it did.

On the last turn, Jane lost her grip, and Cassandra's teeth sank into her lower lip to stop herself from screaming as Jane arced in the air and fell unceremoniously in the dirt.

But an instant later the redheaded cowgirl was standing, a smile on her face. The men circling the corral applauded her ride with catcalls and whistles, expressions of respect.

Forcing her heart to beat calmly, Cassandra tried to dismiss her fright and appear calm. But just as she began to succeed, she saw Kirk mount yet another of the spotted white horses.

This one seemed unusually large, its head high, its ears turned forward in a sign of danger.

Her heart beat faster, but this time not in fear for herself—she was afraid of what might happen to Kirk. Kirk's face showed nothing except the same determination she'd seen in Jane Paulson's.

The moment the horse was released, it rose in the air. Cassandra thought the animal had springs on its feet. She continued to watch, keeping her eyes locked on Kirk, watching the way his muscles knotted as he strained to control and break the horse.

His shirt, soaked through with perspiration, stuck to his torso like a second skin, allowing Cassandra to see the interplay of muscles as he battled the horse. The horse spun and at the same time kicked its rear legs high in an effort to dislodge Kirk. Kirk's hat flew off with the ferocity of the horse's movements, and his wavy hair bounced freely.

Without realizing it, Cassandra was no longer a prisoner of her fears. She was free of them for the moment as she watched Kirk ride, lost within the strength, power, and handsomeness of the man.

Her heart sang its special song to her and brought out all the feelings she had been trying to hide and avoid since the first moment she'd faced Kirk in the lobby of the office building.

As she watched him she forced away those unfamiliar emotions, refusing to allow them a perch within her heart, where they might grow and blossom and only cause her more hurt and anguish.

Instead she concentrated on the determined set of Kirk's strong jaw, which added to the overall picture of total control and mastery he exuded. And, for the five minutes that this particular session lasted, Cassandra knew no time.

When the horse stopped bucking and whirling, and Kirk

rode it once around the corral, Cassandra returned to reality. As Kirk rode past her his eyes fixed on her, and their brown depths pierced her to her very core.

Dismounting, Kirk turned to one of the men. "Take over here," he said. Then he looked at Cassandra. He hadn't seen her when he'd mounted the horse, but when he'd finished the ride, his eyes had fastened on hers and he'd seen her wide-eyed stare. It took all his effort not to show his surprise.

Walking slowly, Kirk went over to Cassandra. "Enjoying yourself?" he asked.

"Learning. Isn't that what I'm supposed to be doing?" she asked, hating herself for using her coolness as a defense while her body burned at his closeness.

"Yes, as a matter of fact," Kirk conceded.

As they spoke Cassandra had become aware that the low rumble of the men's voices had dwindled away and intuitively she knew that they were all looking at her, sensing a confrontation between her and Kirk.

But then she saw Kirk glance around. "I didn't know this was a holiday," he snapped, his voice loud and commanding. One by one the men returned their concentration to the corral.

"Let's go someplace where we can talk, all right?" he asked.

"Fine," Cassandra replied.

Kirk called to one of the men, turned, and whispered in his ear. A moment later the man left, and as he did, Kirk nodded to Cassandra. "We'll take a ride," he added.

"I'd like that." It was true, Cassandra thought. Perhaps alone they could work out their difficulties and make a stab at running the ranch together.

Kirk guided her away from the corrals and toward the

stables, where Cassandra saw several Land-Rovers parked. She saw, too, the ranch hand Kirk had spoken to disappear into the stable.

"What did you think of the horse-breaking?" Kirk asked, his eyes studying her face openly.

"It was . . . exciting," she replied, thinking not of the horses, but of Kirk as he had controlled the powerful animal. "I'm just surprised that there isn't more to it."

Kirk laughed. "That's only the beginning. The first ride. This will happen a lot more, until each mount is fully broken and responds well to a rider. These particular horses will be sold to dude ranches. They have to be as well-broken and trained as is humanly possible."

"I see," Cassandra said, although she really didn't. From the corner of her eye, she saw Jane Paulson walking toward the stable and was about to ask Kirk for an official introduction when he spoke first.

"Cassandra, I'd like you to meet Suzi."

Cassandra turned, surprised for the moment as she saw the ranch hand walking toward them with two saddled horses.

"Suzi?" she asked, her mouth dry again.

"Pretty, isn't she?" Kirk added with a gentle smile as the man reached them. "She's your mount."

"But I thought we were—"

"Going for a ride. Come on, I'll give you a hand up," he said in a friendlier tone than he'd used in the last four days.

Once again Cassandra froze as she stared into the large eyes of the horse. Eyes that she was sure were measuring her for a coffin. She tried to speak, but no words came. Her stomach lurched violently, her head spun, and all the blood drained from her face. "I. . . ." She tried again, but nothing came out.

She shook her head and took a shaky step back. Her eyes went to Kirk, pleading silently, begging for his understanding and help. All she saw were his features turning into a stoic mask.

Kirk watched her strange reaction and felt his emotions turn to disgust once again. She had refused to meet him halfway after he had tried, against his better judgment, to help her. Then his anger gained the upper hand, and he stepped close to her. When he spoke, his voice was low, but his fury was tangible.

"What the hell is wrong with you? I've been patient, damned patient! And you won't give an inch, will you? You're supposed to be here to do a job, and the only way you can is by working with me. But you won't, will you? I don't think you give a damn about what happens here, not one little bit!"

As soon as the first angry word was out, Cassandra had backed away even more. Kirk, his face only inches from her, followed her relentlessly, his accusations stabbing her with knifelike intensity.

"This isn't one of your jet-set resorts. I'm trying to make this ranch work, and I thought that's what you wanted, too. But I was wrong, wasn't I? Perhaps my first impression was right: Maybe all I am is a baby-sitter for a spoiled brat!"

Cassandra reeled under Kirk's ferocious assault, her mind spun, and her heart was torn apart with pain. She shook her head, denying his words, but over his shoulder, she could still see the horse staring at her, waiting for her.

Unable to stand any more, Cassandra whirled away from him, tears brimming her eyes, and ran blindly from the stables. She raced across the road, not stopping until she reached the safety and sanctuary of her suite. Once there, she threw herself across the bed, her body drawing in on itself as she let free the low moans of pain and despair that had been waiting, walled up within the very core of her mind, to be freed.

"Way to go, boss man," Jane said sarcastically.

"Don't start with me," Kirk ordered, his face a stiff, angry mask.

"I don't know what she said to you, but I definitely heard you."

Kirk turned to Jamie Burke. "You can take them back in." When the ranch hand took the horses away, he looked at Jane.

"I was going to take her for a ride, try to calm things down so we could work together, but something happened. . . . She turned pale and started backing away."

"When?"

Kirk shrugged. "When the horses came."

Jane sighed and shook her head. "Have you ever bothered to ask her if she could ride a horse?"

Kirk stared at Jane without comprehension.

"Kirk, not everyone grows up riding. She's a city girl, remember?"

Kirk looked up and caught Cassandra's fleeing form disappearing around the corner of the main house. "Why wouldn't she say so?"

"Maybe she's afraid to admit it to such a great macho cowboy," Jane suggested.

"Macho—" Kirk bit off the word and shook his head. "You know me better than that."

"But she doesn't, does she? What does she know about you? Does she know you used to change my diapers when you were twelve, after my parents were killed? Does she know that you used to hold me at night and tell me stories about what we would do in the future so that I wouldn't be afraid that you would die, too, and leave me alone?''

"This is different," Kirk said uncomfortably.

"Kirk, to anyone who doesn't know you, you're a gruff, unreasoning, tight-fisted, hard man—"

"—I am not a—"

—"Who is the embodiment of gentleness when he lets his guard down. Think about it, big cousin," Jane said as she turned and walked off to leave Kirk alone with his thoughts.

Cassandra turned away from the mirror, and from her red and puffy eyes. Since she'd run into her room this morning, she had not once left it. She'd lain on the bed as she tried to fight her way back to sanity.

Kirk had been cruel to her, and she'd been defenseless against the force of his anger. She had seen the disillusionment and disdain written clearly on his face.

And through the torrent of his raging words, she had seen the impossibility of her forbidden hopes.

I am a fool! she told herself harshly.

Cassandra stared at the tired and sad face reflected in the mirror. Then her eyes played a trick, and the scornful face of her father floated across the glassy surface.

Suddenly Cassandra knew that her father was winning. "No!" she cried. Taking a deep shuddering breath, Cassandra pushed his face away.

I must fight my fear, she told herself. *I must face myself.*

Grasping onto her emerging willpower, Cassandra refused to think about anything other than building up strength. Turning, she strode through the suite and took the wide stairs down to the front door.

When she stepped into the night, she breathed deeply of

the cool air but did not stop to gaze at the beauty of the sky. She walked straight, her shoulders held stiffly, her walk determined and smooth.

As soon as she crossed the narrow road she smelled the cattle and horses, but did not allow the scents to stop her as she headed toward one of the corrals.

When she reached it, her hands were shaking and she grasped onto the wooden railing with a tight and powerful grip. There was a quarter moon above and, with the aid of its pale light, she peered inside the corral.

Ten white spotted horses milled about, some standing dead still, others walking slowly. One, lying in the center of the corral, tossed its head back and forth in the dirt.

The trembling started in her hands until her whole body shook like an earthquake. Nausea rose upward. Cassandra clamped her teeth together and fought it. Staring at the horses, she tried to calm herself.

Then one of the large beasts turned its head, and Cassandra swore it was staring at her. Her legs turned to jelly; she bit into her lower lip. The horse moved toward her, and Cassandra flinched. Suddenly she was tasting her own blood and realized she'd bitten her lip.

They won't hurt me, she told herself. *They won't hurt me,* she repeated.

When the horse was barely a foot away, she could see its flaring nostrils. Its ears swiveled back and forth, but it came no closer. The warm moisture of its breath settled on her hands, and her heart threatened to stop beating.

"H. . . . Hel. . . . Hello," she finally managed to get past the tightness in her throat.

The horse did not move.

Do something! she ordered herself. Carefully Cassandra

loosened her death grip on the railing and slowly raised her trembling hand.

Still the horse did not move.

She reached toward it, her fingers vibrating, her heart thumping, her breath sharp and gasping. Suddenly her fingertips wavered in the air, a hairbreadth away from the horse. Yanking her hand back, Cassandra leaned against the corral railing for support.

Still the horse did not move.

Nothing happened. Once again she steeled herself to try to touch the animal. Cassandra lifted her hand, this time forcing it not to tremble. She almost succeeded. Slowly, in what seemed like an eternity, she moved her hand.

"Y . . . you won't hurt me, will you?" she asked. As her fingers grazed the soft hair of its nose, that long space between its eyes and nostrils, her breath escaped in a whoosh.

She did not remove her hand. The horse still did not move.

Carefully Cassandra began to stroke the horse's nose, her eyes never leaving the horse's, her breathing forced, her heart still pounding like a jackhammer.

She stayed like that for several minutes, running her fingers up and down the animal's face, until at last her trembling body quieted.

Then her breath caught again as the horse's head moved. But she saw that the horse was merely moving its head in rhythm with her hand, and a nervous giggle broke free. She had survived her first test.

"You like that, don't you?" she asked the horse. The animal took another step forward and Cassandra froze but forced herself to stand firm. The horse snickered loudly and bobbed its head several times.

Cassandra did not take her hand away, nor did she acknowledge the silent tears falling from her eyes. "I did it," she whispered to the spotted horse. "You helped me do it," she told him as she continued to stroke him with her now-steady hand.

Cassandra did not wonder at the strangeness of the horse, or why it stood so patiently. Her only thoughts were that she'd broken down the first barrier and that would let her take another hesitant step forward.

She stayed there, petting the horse for another five minutes before stepping back and wiping her wet cheeks with the back of her hand. She smiled at the horse, who still watched her, and then turned, her breathing light and natural once again.

Kirk had been sitting on his porch thinking about the earlier scene with Cassandra, replaying it over and over in his mind, and trying to deny Jane's accusations. Although he still felt justified in his anger toward her, he wondered, as he had in Wyoming, if he was acting out of self-disappointment once again.

Before he could reach a conclusion, he'd seen Cassandra walk between his house and the main house and held his breath as he watched her. He wondered where she was going but did not follow her.

As he tried to think about her in an objective way, his mind grew clouded again as desire and emotions fought with common sense. Her beauty engulfed him, teased him, and haunted him, even as his ever-logical mind refused to be lulled by these visions.

Suddenly he could no longer keep his private battle inside and stood, staring at the spot where Cassandra had disappeared. He left the porch and followed her and just as he reached the road, he saw her walking toward him.

He knew she hadn't seen him: her gaze was fastened to the ground before her. He waited until she was almost on top of him.

"Why?" he asked, breaking the silence of the night.

Cassandra jumped, her heart thumping at the unexpected voice. She raised her head and found herself staring at Kirk.

"Excuse me," she said, again hiding behind her protective coolness.

"Why are you here? You don't like it here, you don't belong here!"

Cassandra shook her head slowly but did not take her eyes from his. "I told you why. I have to be here."

"Really? Isn't the truth simply that your father wants you out of his hair?"

Cassandra's anger surged, but she held it back, aided by the small victory she had just won in the battle for her life. "In a way you're right," she said. Then she looked past him and started away.

She was conscious that he was following her but acted as if she were alone. Finally she felt his hands grasp her arm and spin her around.

She stared at him, keeping her face blank.

"Do you know what you're doing to me? To the ranch?" His hand was tight but he was not hurting her.

Once again, although his anger was plainly written on his face, Cassandra felt the burning power of his touch begin to invade her body and thoughts. His words, too, had a strange and puzzling effect, and her barrier of cold aloofness began to crack.

"Kirk . . . I . . . I know you don't approve of people

like me—that you don't like me. But I have a job I have to do.''

"Don't presume to know what I like or dislike," he snapped, his eyes piercing.

"You didn't have any trouble telling me what you thought of me today, damn you!" Cassandra retorted as she stared defiantly at him.

A tense silence filled the air between them and as it grew thicker Cassandra felt his heady masculine aura begin to envelop her. Her lips were dry, and she flicked the tip of her tongue across her lips to moisten them.

"Why do you hate me?" she whispered when she could no longer stand the silence.

Kirk watched the way her tongue darted across her lips and felt the sorrow that was filling her eyes.

"I don't hate you, Cassandra," he said, "and that's my problem." He released her arm but did not step away.

Their eyes met again, and both Cassandra and Kirk understood what had been said, and what had not. Then Kirk, his eyes sweeping across Cassandra's face, took a single step and closed the distance between them. Even as he moved, Cassandra did, too. Their arms wound around each other at the same instant in time. Their mouths met, and their tongues entwined in a dance of welcome that left them shaken and holding each other tightly for support.

Chapter Nine

Cassandra didn't know how it happened but from the instant their lips met, her world became a whirlwind dream that lifted her from where she was and brought her to where she wanted to be—in Kirk North's strong arms.

The kiss lasted an eternity, and when it ended and she was breathing again, she gazed into his soft brown eyes and knew she could not fight any longer. Her heart had finally overruled her mind and taken charge of her actions.

Miraculously, she could see by Kirk's face, the very same was happening to him. Their mouths joined again, and Cassandra's heart raced madly. Deep within her, a fire rose, consuming her with its intensity and freeing the very thoughts and hopes she had been holding behind locked doors. From the moment she'd looked into his face, she knew the truth could no longer be denied. She had fallen in love with Kirk.

After drawing his lips from her soft, molten mouth,

Kirk's mind spun dangerously. He hadn't planned on this meeting. He knew it shouldn't continue. He tried to stop. He failed. His passions, so tightly controlled since he'd met her, broke free to race wildly through his body.

"Cassandra . . . we can't . . ." he began, even as he lowered his mouth to hers and tasted the warmth of her being.

"We can't fight anymore," Cassandra whispered, as the fire of his kiss burned within her breasts.

Again, unable to help themselves, they kissed deeply and passionately. When the kiss ended and their lips parted, they walked away—not in different directions, but together toward Kirk's house, and the soft yellow beckoning light of the doorway.

The world was a hazy collage of indistinct shapes by the time they reached the porch. But when Kirk paused upon the wooden slats, Cassandra sensed a new hesitation and lifted her head to look at him. She saw that his eyes asked the question his lips did not form. She answered him with the lightest of pressure from her hand on his.

Stopping inside the front door, Kirk turned Cassandra to face him. As he stared at her his chest grew tighter, and his desire rose swiftly, yet he knew he must enforce some self-control. "Cassandra . . . I've wanted you since I first saw you. But . . ." he began.

Cassandra feared that if they talked, her own heart would be robbed, and the love that had finally burst forth would become a wasted and futile longing within her. But with that thought came another fleeting, chilling question. Did he feel the same as she? Cassandra prayed that he did.

Her trembling fingers flew to his lips, sealing them against his next words. "No explanations, no excuses. . . ." She wanted to tell him how she felt, but she didn't. Instead she rose up on her toes and kissed him deeply.

The kiss became an explosion without end. His arms went around her, drawing her close to his massive chest. Her breasts were crushed against him, her thighs melting against his own muscular ones, and the hard leanness of his stomach was like a burning fire next to hers.

Her breath escaped in a low stream when he drew back, while her hands tightened around his back, refusing to allow him escape.

"I want you, Cassandra," he whispered, his voice husky and deep.

"As I want you," she told him truthfully.

With a swiftness that took her breath away, Kirk lifted her from the floor and carried her toward their destiny. Slowly Kirk walked through the living room and stepped into the bedroom. No lights were on, but through a skylight in the ceiling came a silver beam of moonlight that filled the room with a gentle glow.

Kirk released her, and Cassandra slid along his length until she was standing on her feet again. Gazing at his face, she saw the intensity of his emotions. Then he bent, and his lips met hers in another explosive, unbearably beautiful kiss.

When they parted, their chests rose and fell in unison. Electricity crackled in the air as their world shrank until all that was in it was each other. Then Kirk reached for her and slowly began to unbutton her shirt.

With his touch, time came to a halt for Cassandra. In a kaleidoscopic flurry of desire, need, and, above all, love, she and Kirk undressed each other, caressing and kissing as they did. Without remembering how it happened, Cassandra was lying on the bed, looking up at Kirk, who was framed within the silver glow from the skylight.

Kirk's mouth crushed hers, and everything fled from her thoughts, except for the powerful man who held her in his arms.

They kissed for endless minutes, their hands slowly exploring each other. Cassandra luxuriated in the feel of Kirk's strong hands, giving herself up to him even as she learned about his lean magnificent body.

When he drew back from her, she cried out at her loss. But his mouth returned to gently kiss the sensitive skin of her neck, even as his hands caressed her full breasts.

Soon his mouth followed his hands, and pinpricks of desire washed across her in maddening waves as Kirk lavished her with his lips, hands, and body.

Cassandra's blood turned to lava; her desires surged upward. She found herself on the edge of an abyss, about to fall in, when Kirk stopped his maddening caresses and lifted himself to gaze at her.

"I don't hate you, Cassandra; I've never hated you." Kirk lifted his hand and cupped her cheek. He gazed at her, his heart beating loudly, his desire swelling toward the bursting point. But he did not move. He just looked at her and drank in her overwhelming beauty. His eyes swept from the green flashes of fire in hers, to her perfectly formed mouth. He took in the graceful lines of her neck before feasting on the enticing swell of her boldly thrusting breasts. Her skin shimmered in the moonlight, and he no longer cared about the risk he was taking. His emotions ruled him, blocking off any discordant thoughts that would interfere with this night.

"You are truly beautiful," he whispered, bending to

taste the softness of her skin. ''Truly,'' he repeated when he raised his head.

Cassandra blinked back tears of emotion. ''Love me, Kirk,'' she whispered, no longer caring if what she was doing was a mistake, for in her heart, she knew, there was no choice.

Cassandra spoke the words that her heart had cried, and when Kirk kissed her, he did so deeply and passionately, yet his mouth was gentle and loving at the same time.

As the kiss lengthened, another fiery burst of passion exploded. Cassandra's hands moved of their own volition, weaving through his thick hair before leaving it to explore the myriad contours of Kirk's back.

His hands flowed across her body, gently seeking and firmly fondling. Wave after wave of intense pleasure cascaded through her body like the ebb and flow of an ocean tide. Electric shocks rippled across her breasts as his lips showered her with love.

Kirk lost himself within Cassandra's silken body; his lips devoured her, his hands explored her, and his eyes feasted on every part of her. And, as he did, he knew he had stepped across the forbidden threshold, but he could not stop himself.

Cassandra's heart beat loudly as she gazed at Kirk's face, lit by the pale moonlight. She raised her arms, beckoning him, and when he moved to her, her breath caught. Then his mouth was on hers as he fit himself to the contours of her silken body.

Her eyes closed when his arms captured her. Her breasts were crushed against him, and her long legs slowly wrapped around his firm thighs. Cassandra's world wavered, and a searing explosion engulfed her entire being as they joined together in a slow and graceful ballet of love.

They were one. Their passions and desires blended together as their bodies had done, bringing them to a high plateau—a special place Cassandra had never known existed. Their cries of love and passion echoed through the night as Cassandra was carried along on a voyage of love that brought tears to her eyes. With each movement of their bodies, new sensations and emotions were born within Cassandra's heart and mind.

Just when she thought she could take no more, another whirlwind of passion lifted them from their special plateau and sent them spiraling upward to the very center of the universe as their love built to a shattering crescendo that left them both breathless and awed.

They lay still for a long time, neither willing to move, both content within their embrace. Cassandra's breathing slowed, but she refused to loosen her tight embrace, even as she buried her face in the warmth of his shoulder.

She didn't realize she was crying until she tasted the salt of her tears. But the tears were not of sadness; rather, they were of joy, for Cassandra knew that her love for Kirk was not only strong but good.

Lying beneath him, unbothered by his weight, the feel of his warm breath washing across her skin brought her back to reality. She moved, and as she did, Kirk lifted himself gently from her, and then lay on his side, facing her.

Studying her face, he saw the dewy trails on her cheek. He bent his head to kiss them away. Then he stroked her cheek and kissed her lips. He tasted her tears in the kiss and drew her closer again.

Neither spoke; neither wanted to shatter the wonderful aura of love that surrounded them. As they lay there

Cassandra, safe within his arms, fell into a light, secure sleep.

Kirk, dressed only in his jeans, stood on the porch and looked up at the sky. His mind was a maze of confused thoughts, and for the first time in a very long time, he was unsure of himself.

After Cassandra had fallen asleep, Kirk had left the bed, put on his pants, and gone outside. Although he could still feel the silken warmth of her skin and the intense splendor of the lovemaking they had shared, his thoughts would give him no peace.

He berated himself over and over for allowing his emotions to rule him. That was against his rules. But as he looked at the star-blanketed sky, he realized that he was not made of unfeeling steel. He was in love with Cassandra, and he would no longer deny that . . . to himself.

But to what end? he wondered. Kirk was, if nothing else, a realist. He loved his work, loved ranching, and would, if everything worked out the way he was planning, buy his own ranch in two years. His plans had no provision for love—especially with the boss's daughter.

He thought about every moment they had spent together since they'd met. He had seen two vastly different people: the cool and calculating, rich and spoiled jet-set daughter of wealth, and the vulnerable, sweet, and sensitive woman of this evening.

Which one is the real Cassandra Leeds? he asked himself. *Is either real?*

Kirk knew he'd put himself into a precarious situation. Cassandra Leeds was not just another woman, she was the daughter of the man who controlled his future. She was a part of that different breed, known for their unending wealth, uncaring attitudes, and their frivolous and casual affairs.

Kirk wondered if what had just happened was a means of entertainment for Cassandra to wile away the next year. Could this be a casual affair for her? he asked himself. They were far too different, he knew, but did not want to admit.

Yet an hour ago none of those things had mattered—only the overwhelming love and desire that had risen so sharply within him as he had gazed into her flashing green eyes.

Standing alone beneath the open sky, grave doubts invaded Kirk's thoughts and clouded his thinking. She was such a contradiction. She changed with every moment, every gesture. Would tomorrow bring yet more change?

Cassandra woke slowly, her mind filled with a thousand thoughts. Tonight her love had come to fruition, and her emotions were riding a crest she had never before felt.

Everything had been so right: the way they had kissed, the way they'd looked at each other, the way they had become one. Although she wasn't a virgin, Cassandra had never followed the path that most of her friends had. In fact, there had been only one other man in her life—Somner Barwell.

Cassandra shook away any thought of him, not wanting to spoil the beauty of the moment, and reached out to touch Kirk. But where his head had been before, her hand found only emptiness. She sat up and looked around the darkened room for him.

Leaving the bed, she slipped on her shirt and went in search of him. She paused in the living room when she saw Kirk's silhouette pass by the front window.

Going to the screen door, she looked outside. "Hi," she whispered.

Kirk turned. He smiled, trying to dismiss his troubled thoughts as he went to her. Even though she'd just woken, he saw that Cassandra Leeds was still as incredibly beautiful as at any other time, perhaps even more so. Suddenly a harsh and heavy weight descended upon him. "Couldn't sleep?" he asked as he stepped inside.

"I missed you," she replied truthfully.

She went to him and wound her arms around his naked back, luxuriating in the touch of his warm skin on her hands. She lifted herself up on her toes, and as she did, his head bent forward, meeting her halfway. This time their kiss did not become an all-consuming explosion: it was a gentle and soft expression of tenderness.

When they parted, Cassandra gazed at his face. "Kirk, I . . ." but she stopped, unsure of what she really wanted to say. She wondered if he would believe her if she told him the truth—if she told him she loved him.

She tried again to speak what was on her mind, aware of how vulnerable she was letting herself become. "Kirk, I never . . ." but again her emotions cut off her words and prevented her from telling him how she felt.

Kirk held himself back, waiting for her to go on, to say something that would make him believe she felt the same as he, but she didn't. *Is this a casual affair?* he wanted to ask but did not. "I didn't mean for this to happen," he said instead.

Cassandra stared at him, trying hard to ignore the forced tone in his voice. A warning bell of danger rang in her mind as she swept her eyes across his face over and over again, trying to read the meaning of his words. "But it did."

"Cassandra," Kirk began, his hands dropping to his sides, freeing her and balling into tight fists. "Life here is different from what you're used to. In order to run this ranch, I need the respect of the ranch hands. . . ."

An icy chill crawled up Cassandra's spine. She took a single step backward, her eyes wide, her head moving slowly from side to side. "And the men don't respect me. If they think you're fooling around with the boss's daughter, they won't respect you, either, will they?" Her voice was cold, her head tilted to one side. Her words shot out at him, whiplike and cold, even as her heart screamed out its own denial.

Kirk went after her, but she retreated further. He shook his head, trying to make her understand. "That's not what I meant—"

"Isn't it?"

"Cassandra, the world you come from is different. You play by different rules. You have different mores."

She wanted to pretend he was saying something else, but she couldn't. "What different mores? Do you think that tonight was a game?"

"I don't know, was it? What are you doing here with me? You're from the jet set. You're wealthy, and you like to play games. Isn't that what this is to you, a game?"

Cassandra felt as though he'd driven a stake through her heart. Shame flooded her every cell.

"Cassandra," he began.

"Don't bother!" she snapped, her head held proudly as she stared at him, refusing to allow him to see her shame, the degradation of having surrendered to her emotions, of having given herself to someone who wanted her without commitment and without love.

Spinning away from him, Cassandra fled to the bedroom, where she grabbed her clothing and dressed as quickly as possible. Before she could put her boots on, she felt Kirk's presence behind her. Whirling to face him, she tried to control her angered breathing.

"Will you let me finish?" he asked, his voice level, his hands still hanging in balled, knotted fists.

"Will you leave me alone? You made your point!" Instead of trying to put on her boots, Cassandra started past Kirk. Before she could get by him, his arms shot out, and his hands grasped her arms tightly.

She stared at him, her eyes unblinking as she waited.

"Damn it, why don't you take the time to look at yourself, see yourself for what you are? Or is it that you think you can just walk into someone's life, take command, do whatever you please, and then ignore their feelings?"

"No," Cassandra said, her voice filled with disgust, "but it's obvious that you do."

Their eyes locked for a brief flashing instant. Kirk's eyes narrowed and his jaw stiffened. Then he released her and stepped back. "I should have known better," he said.

Her mind went numb; her breath hissed. Cassandra walked past Kirk and stepped out into the night. Ten feet away from the house, though, she stopped to look back. As she did, Kirk stepped onto the porch, his tall muscular body outlined by the light from the doorway. "Bastard!" she screamed.

Rage and humiliation gained the upper hand and lent strength to her arm as she lifted and then hurled one of her new boots at him. She didn't wait to see if it hit him as she turned and walked away. Before she took the first step, the sound of shattering glass broke the night. Turning again, the back of her hand covering her mouth, Cassandra saw that her boot had struck the exact center of his living room window.

Cassandra watched the rising sun. She had been sitting in the same chair since she'd gotten back to her apartment. She hadn't bothered to change, she'd just sat and stared. Her tears had dried before the moon had set. Her sobs of anguish had gone, too.

Eventually her tears had given way to a startlingly dark funnel of anger, hurt, and pain that filled her every thought.

Tonight Cassandra had taken a chance: She had risked her heart and been punished for doing so.

No, two risks, she thought, correcting herself and remembering the agonizing trembling minutes she had spent with the horse. She realized, too, that going to the corral and touching the horse had turned out to be the less dangerous and frightening of the two.

How could he have done that to me? she asked herself. *Who the hell does he think he is?* But Cassandra knew the answer.

Kirk North was the general manager of Twin Rivers. He was a cowboy who'd had his authority taken away, given to a woman who knew nothing about ranching.

Kirk North was a proud man, a man unlike any she had ever known. No matter how hard she tried to hate him for what had happened tonight, she kept remembering his face, lit by the soft glow of moonlight as he looked at her. "I don't hate you," he'd said.

"But you don't love me, either!" Then, as had happened earlier that night, she found yet another deep well of resolve from which to draw. She gathered whatever strength and understanding remained hidden within her, and as the sun broke above the horizon Cassandra began to see things more clearly.

She was doing what Kirk had accused her of not being able to do—looking at herself. She replayed what had happened between them and thought about his unwarranted accusation. *How could he think I was playing a game with him? How?*

Cassandra knew with a certainty she felt deep within her soul that from the moment she'd made the decision to try and salvage her life, there had been no game-playing where Kirk North was involved.

As she thought about the night the self-loathing and disgust that was so suffocating in its intensity began to relent as a new determination rose through the mire of her emotions. A determination that made her sit straighter and breathe deeper.

"But you will love me, Kirk North. You will!" Cassandra's mind whirled and her humiliation and shame receded —she was suddenly seeing herself from the outside. She was looking at a stranger, the same stranger that Kirk North and all the other people working at Twin Rivers had seen.

Cassandra didn't like that stranger. She didn't like the arrogant tilt of her head or the defensive set of her jaw. Nor did she like the assiduous specter of fright lurking behind the hazel green eyes. She understood, too, that for others to like her, to respect her, she must learn how to like herself first.

While she examined herself in this rare instant of unblinded truth, Cassandra wondered what had happened to her to make her like this.

Gazing at the sun, she made herself think back to that

long ago time when she had loved life and loved herself as well as everyone around her. She wondered what she must do, not to merely survive, but to live and make her life what she wanted it to be.

At the same time that Cassandra was beginning to see the world without her rose-colored glasses, Kirk, too, was gazing at the leading edge of the sun, lost within his own bitter introspection.

After Cassandra had gone, leaving behind a shattered window, Kirk had dressed completely and walked to the corrals. As he'd stood by the fence, his mind had become a writhing mass of unwanted thoughts.

Unable to merely stand around, Kirk had taken one of the Land-Rovers and driven off into the night. He drove aimlessly about the ranch, not bothering to stay on the roads, cutting across the ranges, his headlights harsh upon the unpopulated earth.

When he'd reached a small butte, he'd stopped the vehicle and gotten out. With the barely perceptible dawn starting to lighten the eastern sky, Kirk had climbed to the top of the butte, sat, and tried to let the beauty soothe his tortured thoughts.

He sat like that for an hour, watching the black sky change as bands of color began to invade the heavens, heralding the coming of day.

But as the dark purple turned to a crimson streak at the eastern horizon, Kirk saw not the beauty but the similarity of that color to his thoughts. The deep crimson was like a swath of blood—a wound that Kirk had opened and then found himself unable to stanch.

He wondered how he could have fallen in love with

Cassandra. Even as that thought rose in his mind, his memory of this night of magical lovemaking flooded him with all its wrenching reality.

But it was not just the haunting memory of their lovemaking that assaulted Kirk; there was also his own unfeeling cruelty. *Or should I call it fear?* he asked himself.

Cassandra had done nothing to warrant his accusation that she was playing a game with him. Yet he had been afraid that everything about her was a facade, a fantasy game that she was living.

He didn't want to believe it, but he could think of nothing else. She said one thing to him yet acted in the opposite manner. She had told him how important it was to make Twin Rivers a profitable business. Yet she refused to learn about ranching in the only way possible—by being involved with every phase.

Kirk shook his head, but his thoughts would not waver from their path. Cassandra always walked with an air of condescension that declared her different from everyone else. When she talked, her voice was as cool as the breeze on the highest mountains.

"Who are you?" he asked the empty land. "Why are you doing this to me?"

Kirk had to believe that Cassandra was playing a game of her own invention. There could be no other explanation because he knew who he was and he knew her, too. She was a child of wealth, used to the finest of everything. He was from a world with different values and needs. And he knew Cassandra Leeds would never fit into his world, never.

But there was one simple thing that was still bothering

Kirk. If he knew all these things about Cassandra, why was he in love with her?

"But that doesn't matter, does it?" he asked the now fully risen sun. Standing, Kirk started down from the butte.

When he reached the Land-Rover, he sat back in the seat and closed his eyes, once again trying to solve the problems that Cassandra Leeds had brought upon him. "I can't do anything," he said.

That was a lie, and Kirk understood it fully. What he could do, and what he had to do, was simple. He had to make Twin Rivers show a profit this year. And to do that, he would have to be as civil as humanly possible to her. He realized that only with the end of the year, would he know if Cassandra Leeds was playing a game with him or not.

Chapter Ten

Cassandra stared out the kitchen window as she had been doing since the sun had risen and the day had begun. She'd watched the ranch come to life and observed the hands leaving the dining room on their way to work.

She'd watched the ranch hands intently, waiting to see Kirk's form, but he never appeared. Long after the hands had left the area, Cassandra continued to stare.

Her mind was a turbulent seething mass of half-formed thoughts. She had tried over and over during the long dawn to understand the events of last night.

Still, as the sun had climbed higher in the sky, she had found no answers. All she knew was that she must somehow succeed in doing the very thing that had brought her here. She must forget what had happened last night and concentrate on today, tomorrow, and the next twelve months. She must keep her willpower strong and channel her desires and emotions into the ability to do the job that had brought her here.

To do that, Cassandra realized, she must become a part of the ranch. Sitting straighter in the chair, Cassandra contemplated this new thought, evaluating it until she began to understand the basic truth of her new discovery.

Intuitively Cassandra sensed she had found the only thing that would make her succeed. Although she'd only been at the ranch for a short while, she had seen how alien to her past experiences ranching was.

It was a business unto itself, and there was no way she could hope to make it a viable business unless she knew more about it.

"You need the respect of the ranch hands. . . ." Kirk had told her last night in his cruel denial of the love she knew they both felt.

". . . and they don't respect me!" She had flung the words at him with all the force of her pain. But now in the light of day, Cassandra knew how true those words were. The ranch hands did not respect her; they couldn't because they didn't know her. They only knew what they had seen.

Cassandra drew in a sharp breath. She knew what the first step had to be. She must continue on the path she'd started last night before her obviously irrational mistake with Kirk. She looked down at her hands and saw them tremble. Shaking her head, Cassandra stood. *I will do it!* she declared to herself.

Fifteen minutes later, dressed in jeans, a light denim workshirt, and boots, Cassandra stepped outside to walk beneath the morning sun.

At exactly nine o'clock, she reached the double doors of the stables, where she saw the ranch hand who Kirk had sent after the horses.

Cassandra spoke, forcing her voice to remain level, just the opposite of her nervous state. "Jamie, would you saddle a horse for me, please. I think it was Suzi?"

"Yes, ma'am," he said with a nod. "That's the one Kirk picked for you."

"Thank you. Could you bring her to one of the empty corrals?"

"Yes, ma'am," he said before turning and disappearing into the depths of the stables. As she watched him walk away Cassandra knew there could be no turning back. A few minutes later Cassandra leaned against the railing of an empty corral, watching Jamie lead the gigantic beast toward her. *I can do it!*

Feeling the moisture build on the palms of her hands, Cassandra wiped them on her jeans. She held her breath when the young ranch hand opened the corral gate and led the horse in. Then Cassandra followed.

"Suzi's a real sweetheart, Miss Leeds," Jamie said as he looked at the new boss, judging her height and seat before adjusting the stirrups. When he was finished, he smiled at her. "She's got a gentle mouth; you won't have to fight with her. She's real easy."

"Thank you, Jamie," Cassandra said, going to the horse and taking the reins from the stable hand.

"Will you need a hand up?"

"I'll manage," she said without looking at him. She heard him walk away but didn't turn to watch. Her throat had a lump in it, and she hoped she wouldn't suffocate.

Her hands were trembling again, but she refused to yield to her unending fears. Instead she lifted her hand and began to pat Suzi's cheek. "Good girl," she whispered, her voice breaking on the last word.

She patted the mare's cheek for several more minutes, waiting for her terror to recede. When she felt a little calmer, she grasped the reins tightly and began to walk around the corral. Suzi followed obediently, and Cassandra breathed a sigh of relief.

Do it! she ordered herself. She tried, really tried, but the shaking started again and the terror that had developed over the years filled her mind with a black horror that stole her breath from her lungs. Trying to ignore the fright that tried to claim her, Cassandra placed her hand on the saddle horn and lifted her left foot into the stirrup.

Now! she commanded. Gritting her teeth, she pulled her body up. As she did the horse backstepped. Cassandra wanted to scream, wanted to let go and run, but she didn't. She threw her right leg over the saddle, sat down quickly, and gripped the pommel with her right hand.

The knuckles of her hand turned white from the pressure she used to hold on. Thankfully the mare stood still beneath her, and Cassandra let out her breath and opened her eyes. *I did it,* she said to herself. *I'm on a horse.*

She fitted her right foot into the stirrup. One by one she made her fingers loosen their death grip on the pommel and took the reins in both hands. It had been eighteen years since she'd been on a horse, but her hands reacted to the reins as if it had been yesterday.

Her knees clamped much too tightly on the saddle, but that was the least of her worries. Carefully, using the lightest of touches, she pressed her heels into Suzi's flanks and loosened the reins.

The horse began to move; Cassandra's heart threatened to stop. Her body froze and her thighs shook from the pressure she was exerting. When at last she pulled back on the reins, the mare obediently stopped. "G . . . good girl," Cassandra whispered.

Now what? she asked herself.

"Just take it easy," Jane Paulson ordered as she entered the corral and walked over to Cassandra and the horse.

Cassandra looked at the ranch hand in a combination of surprise, embarrassment, fear, and not a little envy. She wondered, too, why Jane Paulson was in the corral.

"If you didn't know how to ride, why didn't you just tell that to Kirk yesterday?" she asked.

Cassandra shrugged her shoulders helplessly, realizing that Jane had offered her a valid excuse that would save her from having to admit the truth. "I don't know."

"All right," Jane said with a shake of her head. "Get down."

Cassandra, still clutched with fear, did not waste a moment in following Jane's instructions. When Cassandra was on her feet and facing her, the ranch hand began to talk in a low, friendly voice.

"Let's start at the beginning," Jane said logically.

A few moments later Cassandra came to the surprising realization that Jane Paulson was befriending her. It took her another few minutes to adjust enough to this startling revelation and concentrate on Jane's voice.

While she listened she began to understand that Jane was teaching her not only about riding but about horses, too. For the next half hour, Cassandra paid close attention to everything Jane said and began to relearn all the techniques she'd hidden in that dark corner of her mind.

When Jane finished her short lecture, she gave Cassandra a look of reassurance. "You do have courage. Not many people would try to ride without someone to help them."

Cassandra nodded. "I had to try by myself."

"But you shouldn't. Until you're very sure of yourself, you should have someone close by. Want to try a few circles?"

Cassandra nodded her head in acceptance.

"Okay. First take the reins in your left hand. . . ." Cassandra followed Jane's instructions to the letter, concentrating intently on the woman's words in order to forget her fear. Before she realized it, she was on the mare again and walking around the edge of the corral, controlling the horse with her legs and hands.

"Very good," Jane said from the center of the corral.

Cassandra rode for a half hour more, until Jane called a halt to the lesson. "I have to get back to work," she said as she helped Cassandra dismount.

Once again on solid ground Cassandra was able to smile. "I . . . I don't know how to thank you," she said.

"Then wait until you do," Jane replied, her smile softening the words. "Would you like me to teach you to ride?"

"Can you spare the time?"

"I can work it out," Jane stated.

"I'd like that very much, only . . ." As soon as she hesitated, she saw Jane tense, so she continued quickly: "Only I would really appreciate it if this could be kept between us for now."

Jane studied Cassandra's face, wondering at the strange request, and decided that there were probably reasons that were none of her business. "All right. Tomorrow morning, same time?"

"Thank you," Cassandra said, her voice filled with emotion.

"You're welcome, Miss Leeds."

"Cassandra, please."

Jane smiled again. "You're welcome, Cassandra."

That afternoon Cassandra straightened up her office, looking through everything, and familiarizing herself with the operation of the office staff, aided by Thelma Westmore, the office manager. By seven o'clock that night, Cassandra was thoroughly exhausted from a combination of lack of sleep, the busy work of the afternoon, and her first time on a horse since her accident.

When she left her office, she saw Kirk sitting at the desk at the far end of the main office. She stopped and realized he was looking at a computer screen. Her heart raced, and her hands balled into tight little fists.

She tried to be quiet, but Kirk must have sensed her presence, for an instant later she was looking into his eyes.

Kirk half rose as he stared at her. "I thought everyone was gone," he said.

"Not quite."

Kirk sighed and finished standing. He walked toward her, stopping a good five feet away. "Cassandra, about last night," he began, but Cassandra cut him off.

A vein pulsed in her neck, and she tried to quell the churning in her stomach. "There was no last night. It never happened. Will that satisfy you?" she asked, unable to keep the pain out of her voice.

"No. But there are two choices for us. We have to work together for the next year, but we can't work like this," he told her honestly. "So either we go on fighting, or you take a vacation for a year and let me run everything. I won't tell your father."

Cassandra heard him but refused to listen. "I'm afraid

we don't have two choices. We have no choices at all. I'm here to do a job, and I won't be chased away. Either you work with me, Mr. North, or I'll . . . I'll damned well do it by myself!''

Kirk studied her face and saw once again the steel band of determination that he'd glimpsed several times before. ''If that's the case—''

''It is!''

''Then if we're going to make it work, we need ground rules.''

''Of course *you* do. What are they?''

''You run the office. You make sure everything goes smoothly on this end. I'll take care of everything that happens on the outside. Any deals for cattle or horses we work on together.''

''Fine,'' Cassandra said tersely.

''I want the books managed tightly. No extra expenses. Double-check and triple-check everything. I'll give you the ordering requisitions. You find the best prices. Manage the ranch, Cassandra, as if every penny we spend is a year of your life.''

''It very well may be,'' Cassandra said in a faraway voice as the reality of her purpose here returned in full force.

On the morning after her talk with Kirk, Cassandra began to drive herself relentlessly. The days flew by, aided by Jane Paulson's riding lessons and Cassandra's total immersion in her work.

By the end of the third week, Cassandra was feeling more comfortable on the horse, and although her fears were still a constant part of her daily battle, they were slowly receding.

When she wasn't riding with Jane, she was either sitting behind her desk working out projections for the ranch or touring in a Land-Rover by herself, checking over the property. Although her agreement with Kirk was for her to stay in the office, Cassandra needed and wanted to learn more. She did, but she made doubly sure never to interfere with him or get too close. She accomplished that very simply. She just drove to wherever there was work being done and sat on the hood of the vehicle, watching from a safe distance.

Several times she'd been aware of Kirk looking at her while he worked. His glances were at times fleeting, at other times so intense she thought she would fall apart.

Whenever they were forced to be together, they were civil to each other in the extreme. Cassandra had decided that showering him with angry words was not the answer. If Kirk was too dense to see the truth of her emotions, she would not try to beat them into his mind.

Instead Cassandra made it a point to be always easy and friendly when he was near. But that, too, was a rare instance. As deeply as Cassandra had thrown herself into her work, she saw that Kirk had done the same. He was rarely around but when he was, it was to sign work orders or hand in inventory requests.

To Cassandra the ranch was like an armed camp with only one side—theirs. Everyone viewed her with suspicion —everyone except Jane.

In the weeks that passed, Cassandra began to look forward to her riding lessons, not because of the riding, but because it was the only time when she had a friendly face to look at and a warm voice to listen to.

By the end of the first month, Cassandra was starting to feel comfortable at Twin Rivers—comfortable, but still not a part of the ranch or part of the people who lived on it.

That fact was driven home on the morning of the start of

her fifth week in Arizona. It was another azure morning. The sun was strong, baking the earth with its hot rays as she walked to the corral where Jane waited with the horses.

"Good morning," Jane said with a smile.

"It seems like it," Cassandra replied.

"Ready?"

"I . . . I guess so," she answered, looking at Suzi. Once again her palms became damp. Today would be the first time Jane was taking her away from the safety of the corrals or riding arena and out onto the ranges.

With her heart beating faster, Cassandra mounted and held the mare in check. Then she watched Jane mount quickly, flash a smile, and nod her head. Cassandra's palms grew even damper, but she kicked Suzi's side gently and guided the mare out of the corral.

They walked the horses for ten minutes, until the buildings were far behind them. Then Jane picked up the pace, urging Cassandra to put Suzi into the smooth-gaited lope she had shown her.

Cassandra complied, her knuckles white on the reins as she made Suzi pick up speed. "Rock!" Jane ordered.

Cassandra followed Jane's command. She moved in the saddle, rocking her hips and pelvis in rhythm with the horse. As soon as she did, the bouncing stopped, and she felt herself become a part of Suzi's powerful strides.

They went on for endless minutes, riding side by side until the tension ebbed from Cassandra's body. A new feeling emerged in its place. Her hands grew steadier on the reins as her legs relaxed and her muscles unknotted miraculously. She felt the return of a confidence that had been driven from her years before. She felt comfortable, almost as if she were one with the horse.

Although all her fear had not fled, enough had departed

to allow her to enjoy the ride. She felt the wind tug at her long hair and felt, too, the strength in the horse beneath her. Without realizing it, a smile was on her lips, and with it came yet another release of tension.

"Beautiful!" Jane declared, watching the change come over Cassandra. If she hadn't been watching, she would never have known the surge of pleasure in helping and teaching another.

The full smile that covered Cassandra's face reached all the way to her eyes. Jane nodded thoughtfully at the comfortable way Cassandra sat the saddle. Her hips flowed effortlessly, her back was perfectly straight, and her arms were relaxed while she handled the reins.

Reaching a small hill, Jane drew back on the reins, and Cassandra followed suit. Cassandra looked at Jane and smiled. "That was wonderful."

"It was, wasn't it. There's nothing to compare, nothing," she said as she dismounted.

Cassandra did the same, and as they walked she looked toward Jane. "Is that why you do it? Work on a ranch?"

Jane wondered for a moment if the question was more than Cassandra being polite. "That's only a small part of it. I grew up and spent most of my life on a ranch. There's a feeling, a sense of belonging, that you can't find anywhere else, doing anything else."

Cassandra heard the deep well of emotions from which Jane drew her words and felt a touch of understanding—just enough to envy the woman. "Have you ever done any other kind of work?"

Jane's short bitter laugh caught Cassandra off guard. "You might say that. I graduated from the University of Arizona with a degree in psychology and interned in a clinic while working toward my masters at night."

"What happened?"

"Nothing. I missed the land, missed the freedom and the feelings that are part of all of this," she said, sweeping her arm in an arc that covered everything they could see. "I left what most people call the real world and came back to the world I know and love. Too much reality destroys people; I didn't want that to happen to me."

"I don't think that could ever happen to you, Jane, you're too strong a person," Cassandra declared.

Jane gazed at her for a long moment before speaking. "Thank you, but I only wish that were true."

"Tell me what it was like to grow up on a ranch?"

Jane shrugged her shoulders. "About the same as anyplace else, except that instead of bicycles we rode horses. Instead of going to a lot of movies and stuff, we took overnight camping trips."

"That sounds like a lot of fun."

"It was."

"Did your parents own the ranch?"

"My father and my uncle. We had two houses—mine and my uncle's. . . ." Jane tried to keep the sadness out of her voice but failed.

"Yes?" Cassandra asked, unable to stop the question from escaping although she was aware that she was treading on forbidden ground.

"It's all part of the past now," Jane said, shrugging and trying to hold back the unexpected moisture that filmed her eyes.

"I'm sorry, I didn't mean to pry. I . . ." but Cassandra stopped when she saw the emotion on Jane's face.

"It's all right," Jane said, regaining control. "It's been a long time since I've spoken about my parents. They were killed when I was still in diapers. I don't remember them clearly. My father, mother, and my uncle were in a horrible automobile accident. I was raised by my aunt and my cousin. In fact, my cousin put me through college.''

"I'm sorry," Cassandra said in a low voice. "What happened to the ranch? Why are you here instead of being there?''

"We lost the ranch. Everyone tried, but without my father and Uncle Burt, we couldn't make it. My cousin was twelve. He tried, but he didn't have the experience. We sold off most of the land but kept a few acres for ourselves, along with the houses and the barn.''

Jane stopped and turned to look at Cassandra, who was gazing at her with a combination of sadness and warmth. "But that's all in the past. Ready to head back?''

Cassandra nodded her head. "Were you very close to your relatives?''

Jane smiled, and Cassandra saw the love within it. "Very close. My aunt died when I was almost thirteen. My cousin continued to take care of me. But when he joined the army, he made arrangements for me to live with a family we knew who had a large ranch. When he got back and started college, we lived together again. He raised me . . . he's as much a father as a cousin. He's—'' But Jane stopped herself before speaking Kirk's name, knowing it wasn't the right time for that.

"He sounds like a wonderful man. I hope I can meet him one day. . . . It must have been nice to have someone who loved you be around as you grew up. . . .'' Suddenly Cassandra turned away. She shook her head and then forced a smile as she mounted Suzi.

Jane followed suit, disturbed by Cassandra's sudden change in mood. But she knew that if and when Cassandra was ready, she would tell her own story.

The ride back was as relaxing as the ride out, and Cassandra allowed herself to forget her problems and even her fear as she lost herself within the moment, relishing and luxuriating in the ride, and in the fact that she was once again on a horse.

When they returned to the ranch, Cassandra and Jane walked their horses until the mounts were cooled down.

Then they led the horses to a trough, and there Cassandra turned to Jane. "I can't thank you enough for all the help you've given me . . . and . . . for being so friendly," she began. It was true, and for the last twenty minutes she had been thinking of a way to repay Jane.

"You're welcome, Cassandra. I've enjoyed it myself."

"Would you come to the office with me for a moment?" Cassandra asked, deciding on a nice way to repay Jane for her kindness.

"Sure," Jane said.

A moment later Jamie came to collect the horses, and the two women went to the main house. Inside, Cassandra led Jane to her private office—Kirk's old office—and motioned her to a chair. When Jane was seated and Cassandra was behind her desk, she opened the large corporate checkbook and wrote out a check. Once she was finished and the check was torn free, she looked at Jane and smiled.

Rising from her seat, she walked over to Jane and handed her the check. "As I said, I can't thank you enough for helping me, and I do hope you'll accept this bonus as a measure of my gratitude." Cassandra knew the words sounded hard and stilted, but she thought that Jane would understand.

What she wasn't prepared for was Jane's instantaneous anger as she looked from the check to Cassandra.

Jane stood slowly, her body tense and stiff. She stared at

Cassandra and then lifted the check. Even as her eyes locked on the other woman's, her hands moved, and the sound of paper tearing was loud in the room.

"I can't believe how stupid I am. I can't believe how much of a gullible fool I was. Who the hell do you think you are? Do you think you can buy anything you want? Is that what life is to you, a check?" Jane's voice was low, but her words cut through Cassandra like a swordstroke.

Cassandra backed away, denying Jane's words with a slow shake of her head.

"I felt sorry for you. Isn't that a laugh? I thought that if I helped you, you would defrost a little and see what was around you. So much for my psychology training. . . ." Jane stared at Cassandra and saw the incomprehension written on her face. With that look, some of her anger melted.

"I guess you can't help yourself. You're a product of a different environment. Cassandra, go home!"

Cassandra, recovering from Jane's unexpected assault, took a deep breath. "I don't understand. Jane, I thought we were becoming friends. I . . ."

"If I didn't hurt so much, I'd laugh at you. Do you think I talk to anyone who will listen about my past? Do you think I dredge up my life's story to entertain casual acquaintances? Today, Cassandra, I thought we'd become friends."

"So did I," Cassandra whispered, confused by Jane's angry reaction to her gift.

"No, Cassandra; friendship can't be bought."

Cassandra's jaw dropped. For the third time, she shook her head in denial.

"I wasn't trying to buy your friendship, Jane. I just wanted to give you something to show how much I appreciated what you've done. You must believe me; that's all it was."

"That's exactly what I tried to tell you before. We're from different worlds. You use money as a thank-you, we use words, or gestures."

Cassandra blinked back the tears that sprang to her eyes. She had made a mistake, a foolish one that would end a blossoming friendship.

"I . . . I have a lot to learn, Jane, and I need someone to help me. Please don't walk away from me. I . . . I want to be your friend."

For no reason at all, tears also rose in Jane's eyes. She tried to blink them away, but when she saw tears spilling unashamedly down Cassandra's cheeks, hers poured free.

"Damn it all, anyway. Ju . . . just say thank you!"

"Thank you," Cassandra whispered, a tentative smile on her face. But for Cassandra, that wasn't enough. There was one more thing she had to do. Stepping forward, Cassandra pulled Jane into an embrace that spoke more than any words could. "Thank you," she repeated.

Chapter Eleven

Cassandra woke to bright rays of sunlight, the first in three days. For the past few days, the sky had been overcast with periods of rain. But today the sun had once again returned with a regal majesty.

Rising from the bed, Cassandra went to the bathroom, brushed her teeth, and took a quick shower, her last for several days. When she was dry, and the moisture-filmed mirror began to clear, she saw a stranger gazing back at her.

Her skin was bronzed from the sun; the whiteness of her teeth lent evidence to that fact. Also the green in her hazel eyes seemed more pronounced against the darker background. Four months of the Arizona sun had worked this startling change on her face. *If only the same would happen to my heart,* she told herself.

Again last night she'd dreamed of Kirk, the same sort of dream she'd been having almost every night. In her dream, she and Kirk would be together, climbing the myriad heights of love and desire, clinging together against all odds, and admitting their love to the world and each other.

But reality came with the daylight and the loss of that love haunted her. Not once in all the time since their first shatteringly passionate joining had they shared another intimacy.

They were strangers who lived on the same land, worked in the same office, and saw the same things day after day, and pretended that nothing had ever happened between them. For Cassandra, the pain increased with the advent of each new day.

So much had happened to her in the past four months that Cassandra knew she could never go back to being the person she had once been. Surprisingly she did not miss the life she'd left behind.

She had conquered her fear of horses to a large degree and had come to love the open, free life at Twin Rivers. Every day was a new experience, offering her unending glimpses into a new world.

The beauty of the land around her was a constant reminder of her new feelings. Even the ranch hands seemed to treat her with less disdain and, although they did not reach out with welcoming arms, they no longer made her feel like an outcast. She sensed that her friendship with Jane had a lot to do with it, because the people who worked on the ranch respected Jane Paulson. If Cassandra and Jane were friends, it stood for something.

Cassandra was also getting to be very, very good at her job, and in the four months she'd been managing Twin Rivers' books, she had saved almost ten percent of the quarterly budget and spent a good deal less than was spent for the same period the previous year.

But not once had Kirk given her the simplest acknowledgement of her work. Kirk never complimented her; he only asked her to save more, to get more.

Whenever he was near, tension gripped Cassandra, making it impossible to work. All she could do was look at him and try to make her heart stop its endless aching.

Pushing away the thoughts that caused only sadness, Cassandra left the bathroom and began to dress. She pulled on a pair of now well-faded denims and tucked the cotton workshirt into the waist. She buckled the two-inch leather belt that Jane had given her as a present and then put on her boots. When she was finished, she crossed over to the chair and picked up the nylon saddle roll that waited for her.

In the bag was a fresh change of clothing. Cassandra Leeds was going on the fall roundup. She was excited and scared half to death at the same time, but she was going.

When Cassandra learned that all the ranch hands were required to round up the cattle that were being shipped out, she wanted to see what it would be like. She remembered scenes from the westerns, in which all the men lived out on the range, rounded up the cattle, and drove them to market.

Although this wouldn't be quite the same, there was an air of excitement hanging over the entire ranch. When she'd asked Jane, Jane had told her about this special time.

There was a sense of returning to the past that everyone experienced. It was a feeling, Jane said, that was unique. It made you want to stay out on the range forever.

Listening to Jane, Cassandra had found herself yearning to be a part of it. Her only hesitation had been that everything was done on horseback—everything. She would have to work with the hands, ride with the hands, and try to learn and do as much as possible.

It had taken her only one long night of deep thinking to reach her decision. She'd come a long way from being the spoiled and naive city girl who had arrived at the ranch four months before with preconceived ideas that had been stripped away by the harsh facts of this new reality. She could sense the differences that were now part of her. But she was not yet a member of the family, so to speak; she was still an outsider. She wanted to belong—she had to belong—if she was to accomplish what she'd set out to do.

In the end, there had been no choice. That afternoon when Kirk came into the offices, she'd asked him to come into hers. After he'd entered, she'd closed the door, turned to face him, and asked if she could join the roundup. He'd stared at hers, disbelief on his face.

"There are no powder rooms on the range. No baths, no showers. You have to eat whatever is served, and you have to like it. There are no beds, just the hard ground you share with a bunch of sweaty men who are working their tails off. Sorry, Cassandra, this isn't for you."

Cassandra had almost backed off. Almost. She had stared at him, wanting to reach out to touch him, to hold him, but she didn't. Instead she shook her head to emphasize her reply. "I'm going."

"We have an agreement. You're in charge of the office, I'm in charge of the outside. There was a reason for it. You don't know enough about ranching. All you'll do is get into trouble, or get in the way."

"It was your agreement, Kirk," she reminded him. "You made it up. You decided what I would do, and what I would not. Not this time, Kirk. This time I go!"

Cassandra watched Kirk as he shook his head. "This is ridiculous. Cassandra, there are a thousand reasons for you not to go. Besides the dirt, you have to be a hell of a good rider."

"I can ride," she stated proudly.

"I heard that you rode around the corral a few times, but on roundup you have to know what you're doing and know what's going on around you. Last year three men, experienced men, were bitten by rattlesnakes. Do you like rattlesnakes?"

"I must; I'm standing next to a big one right now. I'm going, Kirk!" As she'd spoken she'd watched Kirk's body tense. His eyes had narrowed at her insult, but she'd refused to back down. Before he could say anything else, she spoke.

"Who the hell do you think you are? You can take your egotistical, macho, demigod attitude and stick it up—"

"You're not going, Cassandra," Kirk stated again, cutting her off before she could say any more.

"Your nose!" she spat, finishing what she had started. "I'll be ready the day after tomorrow. That is when you ride out, isn't it?"

Without giving him a chance, Cassandra had walked to the door, opened it, and stormed out. Only when she was halfway across the outer office, and she saw the curious stares of the three women at their desks, did she realize that with her grandstand play, she had walked out of her own office, not his.

Kirk stopped his horse on a low rise and surveyed the scene spread out below him. It was a picture-perfect dusk of coral shades blending into purple hues. Several thousand head of cattle were being herded together, and while they moved, cowboys picked out and separated the ones that were ready for market.

Off to one side Kirk saw the outrider he'd been keeping a constant check on. Cassandra was riding the flank of the herd, her responsibilities kept to an absolute minimum.

Yet as cautious as he was with her, he had found himself surprised by her ability to ride and by her dogged determination to do her share. He had not expected that to happen. He had thought that once she realized the hardships of a roundup, she would head back to the ranch. He'd even made sure that there was a vehicle available for her to drive.

But she hadn't turned and run, she had waded in, all inexperience and awe, fighting to keep her head above water. She had not only succeeded, but if she kept on, she might even earn some grudging approval from the men. Maybe.

As he thought about Cassandra, his eyes didn't leave her. She was moving at a steady lope, when suddenly her horse stumbled. He tensed, but then saw that everything was all right and she was still on the mare's back.

But it wasn't, he realized, when Cassandra and Jane dismounted to look at Suzi's front leg. Digging his heels into the horse's flanks, Kirk urged the mount into a quick gallop. A few moments later he, too, was looking at the mare's fetlock.

"She stepped in a chuckhole," Jane began.

"It was my fault," Cassandra said quickly.

"It was no one's fault. These things happen. She'll be okay after a couple of days' rest. You'll have to ride another mount tomorrow," Kirk added.

Cassandra nodded, surprised at the lack of anger in his voice.

"Jane, you'd better give Cassandra a ride back to camp. We're about finished for the day, anyway."

"Yes sir, boss man," Jane replied with a smile. Once she was mounted she offered Cassandra her hand and drew Cassandra up behind her.

With Suzi's reins in her hand, Cassandra wrapped her

free arm around Jane's waist, and they started back to camp, Suzi trailing lamely behind them.

"I feel like a fool," she told Jane.

"Why, because your horse stumbled? At least you stayed on her back. That's an accomplishment."

"When I felt her stagger, my legs locked so tight you would have needed a crowbar to get me off," Cassandra admitted. Part of what she'd said was the truth. She just didn't say how quickly her heart had reached her throat, and how a vision of a nine-year-old girl, hurtling along the ground, her foot caught in the horse's stirrup, had lent strength to her legs and balance to her body.

By the time her horse had recovered its footing, the fear had begun to drain. That, and the fact that she had not been thrown off, gave a boost to her flagging courage.

"We'll find a good horse for you in the morning," Jane promised.

"A gentle one."

Jane laughed as she nodded her head. "Did you really call him a rattlesnake?" she asked suddenly.

"What? He told you?" Cassandra replied, surprised.

"Kirk? No, but Thelma overheard the two of you going at it. She couldn't wait to tell me."

"I'm still surprised he let me come along."

"I think he surprised himself, too," Jane added, not elaborating on the fact that she'd had a fight with Kirk when she'd learned he was refusing to let Cassandra participate in the roundup. Finally Kirk had given up, but when he did, he put all the responsibility for Cassandra onto Jane's shoulders.

"You had something to do with it, didn't you?" Cassandra asked.

Jane shrugged. "Well, it's like my cousin once told me. When you have a friend, value that friendship. Do whatever you have to to keep it. Because good friends are hard to come by."

Cassandra smiled. "Thank you," she whispered. "That must be some cousin you have. I'm looking forward to meeting him one day."

"Cassandra, I can't wait for that day," Jane said, trying to keep the amusement out of her voice.

Five campfires lit the night. Sleeping rolls dotted the ground, and the sound of cattle and horses accented the quiet of the night.

It was almost nine, and most of the ranch hands were asleep. Cassandra sat on her sleeping roll and gazed out at the peaceful picture of the camp. Jane, lying in the bedroll next to her, was already in a deep sleep.

Only about eight or ten men sat around the fires, their voices low as they told their stories. Cassandra listened intently.

She had never before experienced days like this. The world that she'd come from seemed to have been made in a different time. She was relaxed, comfortable, and felt close to everyone around her.

Sighing gently, Cassandra looked around the camp again. As she did, she saw Kirk's tall, lean form walking away from the fires. She watched him, her heart aching again, as he disappeared into the night.

Doesn't he see that I'm trying? Can't he try, too? Making up her mind, Cassandra stood and followed Kirk. She left the low light of the campfires and walked into the darkness. She needed to speak to Kirk and to make him understand her.

Pausing for a moment, Cassandra waited until her eyes adjusted to the dark. Eventually she saw Kirk's outline a few yards ahead of her.

Kirk was physically tired, but his mind refused to allow him rest. He had sat by himself all evening, watching the way everyone interacted. By the time most of the hands were asleep, Kirk could not sit still any longer.

Picking up a small pouch, he left the camp for the solitude of the night. He walked about thirty yards away from camp, where he found a small rocky outcrop to lean against.

Usually roundup meant a time of hard work and good feelings. It was a time to forget the little problems as well as the big ones and, for a few days, become lost in a time warp that denied the existence of civilization.

Yet this roundup was different from any in the past, for civilization had joined him in the form of Cassandra Leeds.

He hadn't wanted her to be here. He hadn't wanted the constant reminder that he was in love with someone whom he could never be with. Yet throughout the past two days, he had been hard-pressed not to watch her. His body had reacted with desire and his emotions were at the breaking point.

But he shored up his overtaxed control with all his might. He could see her long black hair flying out behind her as she rode flank, chasing a calf back into the main herd. It had been then that he'd grudgingly admitted to himself that Cassandra had surprised him with her ability to ride and to learn quickly.

But she was still the little rich girl, the spoiled daughter of wealth that could no more live in his world than he could in hers. That one hard immutable fact burned incessantly in his mind.

Taking a deep breath, Kirk opened the small pouch and took out his fixings. He placed a paper between his fingers and poured the brown shredded leaves into it. Quickly and expertly he rolled the tobacco, licking the paper and sealing it with one smooth movement. When he was done, he took out a wooden match, struck it on his boot heel and lit the cigarette. As he shook out the match he blew a fume of blue-gray smoke into the air.

Cassandra watched Kirk fiddling with his hands. She saw him bend and an instant later watched the flare of a match. She saw his face as he lit the cigarette.

Surprised, Cassandra walked toward him. "I didn't know you smoke," she said.

Kirk stiffened at the sound of her voice. "Only on roundup. It's a habit I got into a long time ago. It relaxes me."

That was very true. As a boy, he had watched his father and uncle go through this ritual each night during roundup. They rolled a cigarette and smoked it just before sleep. It was the only time they smoked, too.

"I've never seen someone roll a cigarette before. For a minute I thought I really was in the old West."

"You can be wherever you want," he told her, keeping his emotions on a tight rein.

"Kirk, I know you don't like having me here, but I want to thank you for letting me come." Even as she spoke, the tension grew thicker. His dark eyes were almost invisible, and she could not fully see the expression on his face. *Get away!* she wanted to scream.

"Thank Jane, not me," he said gruffly—too gruffly.

"I already did. But you're still the boss; I have to thank you." Cassandra clasped her hands tightly behind her back as she spoke.

Kirk took another draw on the cigarette as he gazed at her. "We're getting up early. Don't you think you should try and get some sleep?"

Cassandra nodded. "I just wanted to thank you, and . . . and to tell you. . . ." She stopped, the words sticking in her throat. She wanted to tell him she was trying and that all she wanted was for him to do the same. Straightening her shoulders, she stared directly into his face. "I'm trying, Kirk; I'm trying."

Kirk dropped the cigarette and ground it out beneath his boot. When he looked at her, he saw her eyes were still fixed on him. "Go to sleep, Cassandra."

Cassandra shook her head sadly, turned, and walked away.

Kirk stood still until she disappeared, realizing that the words he'd spoken had been forced. He had wanted to pull her into his arms and crush his mouth on hers. *Go home, Cassandra, please,* he said silently.

The day came early, and Cassandra, who had slept fitfully, did not mind getting up. After a breakfast of scrambled eggs, biscuits, and coffee that Lucy, the ranch cook, had prepared, everyone gathered their equipment and began to saddle the horses.

Cassandra, with Jane at her side, approached her new mount. The horse, an Appaloosa gelding, was about the same size as Suzi but seemed to be a more wiry and muscled horse.

"I suppose his name is Thor or something macho like that," Cassandra ventured as she looked the gelding over.

"I think Killer would be more appropriate," Jane joked, trying to ease the tension she heard in Cassandra's voice.

"Very funny," Cassandra replied. "Really?"

"No, not really. He's a spare, for just this situation. He's a cow horse; he has no name."

"Oh . . ."

"But he's a good mount. Just show him who's in charge," Jane instructed as she bent to pick up Cassandra's saddle.

Cassandra beat her to it, and in one smooth and practiced motion, heaved the saddle onto the horse's back. "Very nice," Jane commented. Cassandra heard a note of pride in her voice.

"I had a good teacher."

When the saddle was cinched tightly and her equipment set, Cassandra stood next to the gelding while Jane saddled her horse.

Twenty minutes later they were riding flank on the herd, and Cassandra lost herself in the work, marveling at her newfound sense of freedom and enjoyment. She had exerted full control over the gelding, and by the end of the first hour, was almost as comfortable riding him as she had been with Suzi.

The morning passed swiftly, and when lunch was over, the roundup continued. They had cut the herd to half its original size and were just about finished. Tomorrow they would drive the herd to the pens in preparation for shipment.

By mid-afternoon, Cassandra found herself riding with Jane and another hand. They were on the far flank of the herd when they spotted a lone calf off to the side, acting strangely. In unison, the three riders went toward it. Drawing near, they slowed their horses.

"He's stuck," Jane said, as she started to dismount. Cassandra saw that the calf had caught its hind leg between two rocks and was trying vainly to get free.

The other hand dismounted to help Jane, and as he did his horse seemed to shy away. "Damn!" the man spat as he jumped free of the stirrup.

When he landed on the ground, his horse reared suddenly. Cassandra's gelding snorted, and she felt its body tense.

"Watch out!" the ranch hand yelled, backing away from the slithering reptile which had suddenly appeared beneath his horse.

The air was shattered by the sound of rattles, and Cassandra's heart started pounding. Her horse shied and started prancing away. "Hold him!" Jane shouted.

But Cassandra couldn't. The horse's eyes rolled with fear, and he was suddenly rearing, his front legs flying high in the air, kicking out defensively.

Cassandra fought to hold him back, but the powerful gelding refused to obey her commands and an instant later he was off in a panicked gallop.

Cassandra's heart tried to stop. The blood drained from her head, and tendrils of fear had her in a death grip. She grabbed the saddle horn tightly with both hands, the reins still clutched within them. She held on, fear adding strength to her grip as the horse ran madly out of control.

She was suddenly feeling all the pain of her first accident and knew that at any moment, she would be hurled from the horse's back, crushed beneath him, and then dragged endlessly along the ground, unable to stop, unable to do anything but endure the unbearable pain and agony.

''Help me!'' she screamed, her voice breaking as she called out.

Kirk, as he had been doing all day, continued to check on Cassandra and Jane. But after last night, he wondered if he could keep up his act. *I have to,* he reminded himself.

He saw Jane, Cassandra, and Bill Norton angle away from the herd and turned his attention back to the others. A moment later he spun in the saddle. Intuition, built from years of experience, warned him that something was wrong!

He searched everywhere. Then he saw Cassandra's horse rear, its front legs flying out in a defensive kick.

Before he could move, the gelding spun and took off in a panicked gallop with Cassandra clinging helplessly to its back.

Kirk's heart beat rapidly, and his spurred heels dug cruelly into his horse's flanks, sending it racing forward on a path that would intercept Cassandra. Bending low in the saddle, he saw Jane doing a running mount as she, too, started after Cassandra. Bill Norton was running, too, but he was chasing his horse.

Kirk knew that only one thing could have caused this scene. They had disturbed one of the numerous rattlesnakes in the area.

Kirk urged more speed from his horse as he leaned forward. His mind raced madly as his eyes locked on Cassandra. He refused to think about what might happen.

''Hold on!'' Kirk shouted, knowing full well that Cassandra couldn't hear him. Concentrating with all his power, Kirk kept the pressure on his horse, urging it with his spurs, his hands, and his prayers to go faster.

Two minutes later he saw that he was gaining on her. The

angle he'd intuitively chosen was the right path, and just as Cassandra's horse went down a small incline, Kirk knew he would make it.

But then the cold hand of fear squeezed his heart as he realized where the horse was taking her. Ahead of them was a level valley that they never crossed. The valley floor was not sand and earth but was a bed of randomly strewn rocks that defied anyone to ride across them at a pace faster than a walk.

Kirk knew he had only a few moments left. If he didn't reach her, it would be all over. "No!" he swore defiantly.

Cassandra fought her fear, fought the paralyzing effects that the fear drowned her in, but even though she did, she could not gain control over the powerful horse. Its headlong rush for safety was the only thing that controlled it.

Flecks of the horse's sweat flew into her face, but she didn't even feel it. Her hands were stiff; her fingers ached from their painful grasp. Her stomach churned, and with every stride the horse took, she thought she would die.

Fight! she told herself. *Fight!* She tried, but she could not regain control. The loud sound of the horse's strained breathing reached her ears just as they entered the level valley. Then Cassandra's already pounding heart beat faster. Before her, strewn everywhere, were rocks. The valley floor was composed of rock and stone.

Summoning up whatever strength remained in her arms, Cassandra made herself sit up against the rocking, tossing gait that controlled the horse. She bit down on her lower lip, and as she felt a flash of pain she jerked back sharply on the reins.

The horse's head moved with the reins, but instead of

slowing, the horse continued on its mad charge, its head turned halfway back as it ran blindly toward its death.

Cassandra fought. As she struggled with the reins, she sat further back in the saddle the way Jane had shown her, in an effort to make the horse stop, but it made no difference to the uncontrollable runaway.

A hundred yards ahead loomed the mouth of the rocky valley. Her eyes widened as she saw it rush closer.

"Kirk!" she screamed. "Help me, Kirk!"

And suddenly she saw a man riding next to her, approaching at an angle that would cut off her horse's headfirst run. Cassandra, still held prisoner by her inability to control the horse, saw Kirk responding to her cry.

The world moved in slow motion, and with every bounce she took, she saw Kirk edge closer. With unbelievable clarity, she saw the taut lines of his face and the grim slash of his mouth as he began to straighten up in the saddle.

Fifty yards separated her from death. Twenty yards separated her from Kirk. Inexorably the rocks inched nearer.

Suddenly Kirk was in front of her, his horse cutting hers off, edging it away from the rocks in a wide circle. As Kirk did this Cassandra eased back on the reins, and her horse's head straightened out again.

Kirk reached out and grasped her reins, almost at the bit, and began to slow his horse. A thousand lifetimes later, the horses stopped.

Kirk dismounted quickly and went to Cassandra. He froze for a moment when he saw the chalky pallor of her face and the thin trail of blood that came from her cut lip. He reached up to her, grasping her stiff body and easing her to the ground.

When she was next to him, her eyes still filled with fright, he couldn't stop himself from taking her into his arms and holding her tightly.

A moment later he released her and stepped back. He looked into her eyes and saw life return to them. Then he looked up and saw a half-dozen riders approaching, Jane at their lead.

He freed one arm from around her and waved to them, signaling that she was okay. He was conscious of the concern on Jane's face and nodded to her that Cassandra was all right. A moment later the hands turned their horses and started back toward the herd.

When Kirk looked down at Cassandra again, he noticed that some color had returned to her face. "You're safe now; it's over," he whispered.

Without warning, Cassandra began to shake. Kirk, taken off guard, felt her body tremble violently. He pulled her tightly to him, burying her face in his chest, but it didn't help. He felt her legs fall out from under her, but his arms held her up.

"It was happening again," came Cassandra's muffled cry. "Oh, God, I was going to be hurt again," she sobbed.

Kirk said nothing. He just held her for a long time, until at last the shaking began to lessen.

What was happening again? When was she hurt before? Suddenly Kirk understood her. He remembered that afternoon in Wyoming as they walked to the corral. She had stopped and spoken in a tight, edgy voice. At the time he hadn't realized that he'd seen fear on her face. He had taken it for something else.

Stupid! he called himself, remembering that day when he'd had Suzi saddled and brought out to her. He'd seen her face go tight, heard her voice crack, but had been blind to the pure fright that had suffused her entire being.

He hadn't seen it because he hadn't wanted to. He had wanted to see a spoiled, shallow woman whom he would not want to be in love with.

"Cassandra," he whispered, forcing her to meet his gaze. "I'm sorry."

Chapter Twelve

*H*eld back by her concern for Cassandra, Jane did not immediately follow the other hands. But when she saw Kirk holding Cassandra and saw, too, the look of love and solicitude on his face, she thought that perhaps this wild chase had been for the best.

"Good luck, cousin," she whispered as she started toward the herd.

Behind her, Kirk loosened his grip on Cassandra. "Why didn't you tell me?"

Cassandra took several deep, calming breaths while she tried to organize her thoughts. His words kept echoing in her ears. "I'm sorry," he'd said.

"Tell you what?" she asked finally.

"That you're scared to death of horses. Why?"

Cassandra stepped out of his strong embrace. "Shouldn't we get back?" she asked, avoiding both his question and his eyes.

Kirk shook his head. "When we're ready." Saying that, he turned toward the horses and grasped both leads. "Come," he whispered to her as he started to lead the horses back.

Cassandra watched him approach and, surprisingly, felt no fear when she looked at her sweat-drenched mount. When her gaze returned to Kirk, she felt the chilling memory of that other time, after the accident, when her father had brought her back to the riding club to ride again. Was Kirk going to do the same thing?

"I . . ." But she stopped when she saw the puzzled expression on his face.

"What?" he asked.

"Are you going to make me get on the horse now?"

Kirk heard much more than the question. He studied her intently. "I was thinking that a walk might help."

Cassandra's breath exploded from her chest. "Thank you. It will."

They walked for several silent minutes, and Cassandra began to relax even more. She had survived her worst nightmare, she realized, and was alive, with only some minor pain in her rear end. She almost smiled—almost.

Kirk was alone with his thoughts while they walked. All his preconceived ideas about Cassandra Leeds were falling apart and he was not trying to fight that. He couldn't any longer, especially since he'd thought he might lose her, forever.

"What made you so afraid of horses?" he asked after a few more minutes.

"Does it really matter?" Cassandra asked listlessly, remembering how clearly Kirk had shown that her love was one-sided.

Stopping, Kirk grasped Cassandra's arm and made her face him. "Yes," he said simply.

Suddenly Cassandra's carefully maintained shell collapsed. "All right," she whispered.

For the next twenty minutes Cassandra spoke, telling him about everything that had happened eighteen years before, from the moment she'd gotten on her father's champion horse until she woke in the hospital three weeks later. She told him about the nightmares and the unending, paralyzing fear. When she finished, her face was streaked with tears.

Kirk remained silent for several minutes after Cassandra finished. When he finally spoke, his words were heavily laced with emotion.

"You're a brave woman, Cassandra. Braver than a lot of men I know."

"No, I'm not. I'm just a scared little girl who pretends a lot."

"Don't denigrate yourself. I meant what I said. I'm sorry for the way I've been treating you."

Cassandra's heart fluttered and her stomach churned. His words were warm. But then she wondered if these emotions were just a carryover from the presence of danger.

"Maybe I should try to get on the horse again," she ventured in a low voice.

"Only if you want to." Kirk's words were so different from her father's long-ago, angry orders to a nine-year-old.

"I . . . I want to," she declared in a firm voice.

Kirk unsaddled and tethered his horse and looked around. He saw Cassandra pouring herself a cup of coffee, along with several of the hands. Turning, he started toward two of the ranch hands when Jane stopped him.

"Can we talk?" she asked.

Kirk guided her from the men, stopping when they were far enough away for a private talk. "Go ahead."

"That was a hell of a chase."

"It was close," Kirk replied.

"Can't you unbend a little? You almost killed your horse to catch her. When you did, I saw the way you looked at her. Can't you admit how you feel, even now?"

"What good will it do?"

"You're in love with her. Does she know it?" Jane asked.

"It doesn't matter."

"It doesn't matter," Jane mimicked sarcastically. "Like hell it doesn't. Sometimes I can't believe you're the same man I know and love. The man who has all the answers. The man who knew what to say and how to say it all. You taught me, and that says a lot, but you can't do it for yourself, can you?"

"Not now, Jane."

"Then when?" Jane asked, her eyes boring into his. "When she's gone?"

Kirk shook his head and steadied his nerves. "Even if she did feel the same about me, it couldn't work. We're too different."

"Or too stubborn. She loves you, Kirk."

"She might have once, but not anymore," he said with certainty.

"Kirk—"

"Enough," Kirk stated, ending their conversation by walking away.

"Not enough by far," Jane whispered to his back.

* * *

Cassandra sat on her sleeping roll, staring up into the night. Her mind was constantly shifting, her thoughts not on the afternoon, but on the evening.

What had impressed Cassandra most was that no one mentioned her mishap. Too, she had been included in the random conversations that broke out spontaneously among the ranch hands sitting around the fires.

For the first time since arriving at Twin Rivers, Cassandra had started to feel like she belonged. There was nothing overt in the way it had happened, but she felt it in the little gestures.

However, the one event that brought home a true sense of belonging had occurred just before everyone had left the fire to go to sleep.

Bill Norton, the rider who'd been with them when her horse had been spooked, stood and walked up to her. The men had grown silent, and Jane, who had been sitting next to her, had a shadowy smile on her face.

Cassandra had glanced at Kirk, sitting on the other side of the fire and saw him staring at her.

"Miss Cassandra," Bill had said, his voice rough but easy, "this is the last night of your first roundup, and we . . . the boys, I mean, wanted to give you a memento."

Cassandra tensed but continued to look up at him.

Slowly Bill had slipped his hand from behind his back and held up a tannish object about three inches long. Cassandra had stared at it without recognition, until Bill shook it.

Cassandra jumped. A round of laughter echoed in the night, and as the color had returned to Cassandra's face she'd tried to smile. "This came from that critter that tried to eat your horse,'' Bill informed her as he offered her the rattle.

Forcing a smile to her lips, Cassandra had gingerly and bravely taken the rattle. She'd studied it closely and then looked directly at Kirk. "Doesn't look half as mean as some people I know."

With that, more laughter had erupted around the campfire and Cassandra felt a warmth she had never expected. From the corner of her eye, she'd seen Jane laughing. But at the same time, she'd seen that Jane's gaze was directed at Kirk, whose smile had become taut.

After that, everyone had gone to their bedrolls, including Cassandra. But she had found sleep elusive.

Shaking away her roaming thoughts, Cassandra stood, stretched, and then walked away from the dying fires, a blanket under her arm. She needed to be away from people for a little while.

Kirk lay still on his bedroll, thinking back on Cassandra's sad tale. For most of the day, he'd chastised himself for having always thought the worst of her.

With her story had come a new understanding of who and what she was, and a breaking down of his own false assumptions. He had apologized to her today but wondered if it had been too late.

He knew, too, that if it was, it was his fault. He had been the one who'd passed judgment and set the rules.

When he'd spoken to Jane, he'd been sure that any future with Cassandra was impossible. Yet in the back of his mind, hope still existed.

As his thoughts churned he saw Cassandra, who was sitting a dozen paces away, stand and walk from the campsite. He watched her, knowing that he would have to face her and face himself.

Making his decision, Kirk followed Cassandra into the night.

Cassandra walked slowly, her mind still racing with everything that had happened. But overpowering all her other thoughts was the memory of Kirk's strong arms around her, holding her tight while her body shook in reaction to the shattering ride. She had found, pressed securely to him, that she had been able to draw on his strength and fight for control of her mind.

When she had calmed down and looked at his face, a flood of emotions had filled her body. She had wanted to tell him she loved him, but knew the futility of it. Yet he had been kinder and gentler with her than ever before, and she did not want to chance losing that. It was all she could hope for.

I've been raised to want too much, she decided, feeling a deep sadness at the thought. Kirk had been good for her today; he had been strong when she needed him, and he hadn't forced her to do anything she didn't want to do.

Even when he'd pushed her to talk about the accident, she'd sensed it was for her own benefit. When she'd finished the tale, it had somehow seemed distant, as if it had happened to someone else. Afterward, when she'd decided to try to ride the horse, she found herself nervous but unafraid.

She realized now that by speaking aloud about what had happened so many years before, the words had been cathartic, releasing her from the suffocating bonds of fear.

"Do you hate your father?"

Startled, Cassandra whirled at Kirk's voice, her hand going to her throat. A moment later she lowered her hand.

"Do you hate him?" Kirk repeated.

"Hate him? Why?" she asked, puzzled by the question.

"For sending you here. For preying on your fears in order to take advantage of you. For playing dirty to get what he wanted?"

Cassandra heard anger in Kirk's words and knew that he cared. Her heart beat with a different emotion, and a heavy lump grew in her throat. "You really do care, don't you?" she asked.

Kirk stepped closer to her, and although it was the dead of night, he saw her features clearly. "I care, Cassandra. You know that."

"Kirk . . ." she whispered, closing the distance between them and reaching up to capture his mouth with hers. Her arms went around his broad back, and the blanket, so carefully tucked beneath her arm, fell to the ground.

The world lit with the soaring explosion of their kiss as Cassandra leaned against him. When the kiss ended, they gazed deeply at each other for a long moment, until neither could stand the tension swirling around them.

Kirk's mouth descended again, slowly. This time their kiss was not a soul-shattering explosion of passion—it was a gentle expression of their innermost emotions, a kiss that told of their deepest feelings.

As it had happened that first time, they found themselves lying on the blanket, wrapped in each other's arms. Their bodies joined together, their hearts beating as one as they raced toward the heavens, toward that special place in the universe that was theirs alone.

Later, when their bodies returned to Earth and they could feel the warmth of their joining upon every inch of their skins, they lay together, side by side, their hands constantly moving, caressing each other gently while they shared kiss after kiss.

Even later, after they had dressed, they sat holding hands under the sparkling stars.

"You still haven't answered me. Do you hate him?"

"No, Kirk, in spite of everything, I love my father. I only wish he loved me."

"Are you sure he doesn't?"

"I only know that he did love me when I was a little girl."

"How could he have sent you here, knowing about your fear of horses?"

Cassandra smiled. It was a cold, hard smile. "I told you why in Wyoming. Gregory Leeds likes to win. He wants me to marry Somner Barwell. He wants to arrange some sort of a merger with Barwell Industries."

"He thought you would quit, run away?"

"That stands to reason."

"Cassandra, what about Barwell?" Kirk asked, needing to know the absolute truth.

Cassandra's mouth went dry, her stomach starting its flip-flops. "I won't marry him," she stated. "I don't love him, Kirk. . . . I love you."

The silence that descended was louder than any noise could be. They stared at each other, their eyes sweeping back and forth across the planes of their faces.

Kirk wanted to declare his love for her, but reality intruded once again, and with it came logic.

"Cassandra," he began in a low voice tinged with the sadness of the memory of their lovemaking. "Is love enough for people as different as we are? Our lives are so far apart. Our thinking, our desires—"

"Are they, Kirk?" Cassandra asked, refusing to let his words shatter the love she felt. He had done it once; she would not let it happen again. "Or are you afraid of making a commitment? Are you afraid of being responsible for another person's happiness?"

"Cassandra," he began, but she cut him off quickly.

"You chased me away once. And I deserved it. I never fully took your feelings into consideration. I was just what you called me, a shallow, even callous, and spoiled girl. But have you looked at me lately? Have you really seen who I am now? I've learned a lot, Kirk. I have more to learn, but I'm trying, damn it. I'm trying with all my heart."

Kirk gazed at her, his hand tightening on hers.

Cassandra sighed. "You love me. I knew it that first night we made love, and I know it tonight. You don't have to say anything; it's not necessary. But don't run from me . . . and don't chase me away."

When Cassandra had started speaking, her thoughts had become crystal-clear, and she knew not only what must be said but what must be done.

"I'll be here for you when you need me. I'm yours, Kirk, just as you're mine. Remember that. Besides, you're forgetting something."

"What?" Kirk asked in a thick voice.

"We still have to beat my father!"

"You already have," he told her proudly.

"Not yet. Remember, I said he always hedges his bets. He has other ways to stop us."

"He won't," Kirk promised just as the first thin streak of daylight appeared on the horizon.

Standing, Kirk offered his hand to Cassandra. She took it and pulled herself to her feet. "I love you, Kirk, but that will be between us. I know how you feel, so we won't advertise our doings to the others." Saying that, Cassandra bent, recovered her blanket, and started away. But she stopped after several steps and turned back to look at him.

"Good morning," she said with a smile.

Kirk watched her take several more steps before he finally spoke. "Cassandra."

She stopped, her heart pounding so loudly she thought the whole world must hear it. Slowly, with her breath lodged somewhere between her heart and her mouth, she turned to face him.

"I love you," he said.

Cassandra smiled as her eyes flooded with tears. "It took you long enough to admit it," she told him before turning again and walking back to camp.

Cassandra looked at the cold black plastic telephone and reached for it. It was report time—the third quarterly report—and for the first time in nine months, she was looking forward to talking to her father.

As she dialed, her thoughts flashed back to the time just after the roundup, when the days had spun into weeks and the weeks had blended into months of hardworking days and slow, incredibly wonderful nights that hurtled her and Kirk onward to their destiny.

At the office, Cassandra became more and more adept at cutting corners to save money, while learning how to set prices and read the markets well enough to project accurate figures.

Working with Kirk instead of against him, she had learned more in the space of a few months than most people would have learned in years. Working together, they were able to initiate a wide variety of changes on the ranch.

Even Kirk had been surprised by several of Cassandra's ideas, and after scrutinizing them for hidden flaws, he pronounced them sound.

"What I don't understand," he said one evening as they'd sat in his living room listening to music, "is how you spotted these things when I couldn't?"

"You've lived with them all your life. Because I'm new to all of this, I have to question the why of everything. When I do, I see other possibilities."

"Yes, you do," Kirk had said with a proud smile on his face.

They spent many nights enjoying each other's company, sitting for hours, complacently talking, having no other need than to be with each other. But as their love progressed and the ranch work continued, Cassandra found herself bothered by the way they acted around everyone else.

Although she had agreed with Kirk that they would keep their relationship private from the others, she disliked having to hide her emotions so totally from the world. She had consented to keep their love a secret at the beginning, but as the months passed, Cassandra wondered why it had to stay hidden.

One of the reasons was Kirk's own stubborn pride. Kirk felt that the knowledge of their relationship must remain between them. He believed it would still be detrimental to the ranch if the hands discovered that the general manager and the boss's daughter were in love.

Cassandra, although annoyed with Kirk's reasons, actually did understand them. She found herself praying for the end of the year to arrive and free her of her promise to her father, and free her to declare her love openly for Kirk.

Even though her schedule was jammed, she still found

time to spend with Jane, riding, or just talking. Their friendship was growing even stronger, and Cassandra treasured it. But even with Jane, she did not speak of Kirk in any but the broadest of senses.

So she filled her days with work and found that she enjoyed the business of ranching and the challenges it offered her. One in particular emerged during the monthly staff meeting, which involved Cassandra, Kirk, and several of the ranch hands. The subject of the meeting was the Appaloosa sales.

"We'll just have to wait until we've built up a new herd," Kirk had reiterated.

Jack Slater, the man responsible for the breeding of the horses, spoke up. "I still think it's a mistake not to buy a few-hundred head. If we don't supply anyone this year, the other breeders are going to take our future business from us."

"We've been over that ground before," Kirk said in a tired voice. "It's a chance we have to take. We want everyone, when they think of Twin Rivers, to think of our stock as the best. If we have to buy prime two-year-olds to do that, it will take years to make back the money. We can't afford that."

Cassandra, sitting silently, had listened to the exchange when she had an idea. "May I ask a question?" she offered.

"Go ahead," Kirk said.

"Before I do, let me see if I've got my facts straight. If we can't afford to wait for our herd to mature, and we can't afford to buy horses for resale, then we stand the chance of losing a large amount of future business to our competitors, who will already have made substantial sales to our customers. Correct?"

The five men sitting at the table nodded solemnly.

"Then why not presell the horses?"

"Excuse me?" Jack Slater asked.

"Like the commodity market. Sell a chance on the future. Look," Cassandra had said as she stood. "We need two full years to build the herd up to size. But we also need the money. Everyone here has said, often enough, that the new stud will make our herd the finest in the area. Why not use that? Besides, our other studs are, according to all of you, of the highest quality."

Cassandra had paused to look at each man individually, but only when she reached Kirk's face did she see a hint of understanding.

"It's really quite simple. We go to our best customers, show them the new stud's papers, and make a deal. We give them the projected price per head for both our regular breed stock, and the newly bred stock, but we tell them that if they buy now, the price will be twenty-five percent less. We're asking them to take a chance, but we're giving them the incentive to do so. Next year they'll make do with whatever horses they have to buy, knowing that in two years, they'll get the very best!"

"And," she'd continued, rolling along with the excitement her momentum had created, "with the advance sales, we can buy more brood mares to increase the herd faster."

When she'd finished, she'd seen the surprised looks turn to grudging admiration. But the best reward had come afterward, when she and Kirk were alone.

He'd looked at her, his eyes sparkling. "I knew that you were smart, but I never realized that so much brainpower could be wrapped in such a pretty package."

Cassandra had smiled and remained silent for a moment.

When she spoke, her smile had widened. "Yes, you did," she stated simply.

Cassandra gripped the phone tighter as her thoughts returned to the present and she heard her father on the other end.

"Hello, Father," she said in a level voice.

"Good evening, Cassandra. I've been expecting your call."

"I know you have," Cassandra said, her voice pitched in a haughty, mocking tone as she informed him that the ranch had broken even, according to the figures of the third quarterly report.

"And we fully expect to show a profit by the end of the fiscal year—in three months," she stated proudly.

"I'm surprised," Gregory Leeds said in a tight voice.

"Why? I told you I could do it," she responded.

"How?"

"The horses, Father. The horses."

"What horses? The ranch doesn't have any horses to sell."

"Read the third-quarter report. We sold two-hundred head at nine-hundred dollars apiece. Half down, half upon delivery. That's ninety-thousand dollars in advance! Good-bye, Father. I'll speak to you in three months."

Cassandra hung up the phone and smiled. She was doing it . . . They were doing it. "I love you, Kirk," she whispered.

Chapter Thirteen

The soft strains of a gentle ballad floated in the air. Cassandra closed her eyes and rested her head on Kirk's shoulder. She felt at peace with herself and with the world.

They had just finished another long workday and afterward Cassandra had invited Kirk up for dinner. She had cooked two steaks, which they'd eaten sitting at the candle-lit kitchen table.

The entire evening had been spent in a relaxed, romantic mood that neither wanted to break. And now, resting against Kirk, she felt drawn to his heady masculine aura.

"Dance?" Kirk asked.

Cassandra opened her eyes and lifted her head. "I'd love to. We haven't danced since that night at the . . . Cow Palace."

"Wonderful place, the Cow Palace," Kirk said with an amused grin.

"It was," Cassandra stated in a serious voice as she stood. A moment later Kirk enfolded her in his arms.

They danced slowly, lovingly, and when the song ended, they swayed together, waiting for the next cut of the album to come on.

The world, as was its wont lately, disappeared again for Cassandra, and nothing else existed except for her and Kirk. When the song was over and they stopped moving, Cassandra opened her eyes to find Kirk gazing at her.

"I love you," he whispered as his lips came down on hers and his arms moved in unison. An instant later Cassandra was swept off her feet and carried into the bedroom. "I need you, Cassandra," he said in a husky voice.

Cassandra, hearing the love and desire in his voice, lifted her mouth to his to taste his warm sweetness.

He placed her gently on the bed and slowly undressed her. When she was bared to his gaze, he stepped back and undressed. Cassandra watched him unashamedly, drinking in his every movement, letting her eyes wander freely where they would, knowing that there was no shame in what was happening between them. There could be no shame in their powerful love.

After he was undressed, he went to the bed and joined her, gracefully easing his length next to hers, scooping her in his strong arms and drawing her close while he let the warmth of her silken skin radiate along his body.

Cassandra moved closer to Kirk even before his arms were fully around her. Her sensitive breasts were pressed flat to his chest, and tiny explosions of desire flared within them. Her fingers ran through his thick hair and then traced the lines of muscles radiating from his neck, until her fingertips reached the arching swell of his buttocks.

Their tongues danced together; their hands stroked and explored in a combination of desire and love. Then Kirk shifted, moving Cassandra with him until he was above her. He tore his mouth from hers and let his lips roam downward along her jawline, the heat from his mouth maddening as he reached her neck and the lightly pulsing vein that throbbed just beneath the surface of her skin.

His burning lips heated her blood further. Her fingers roamed across his back as his mouth incited her. She cried out when he took his mouth from her throat and cried again when he captured the stiff tip of her breast.

Lances of fire burned her nerve endings, and her need for him grew out of control. When he graced her other breast with the demanding heat of his tongue, her hands returned to his hair and she pulled his head up, forcing his lips to hers.

Cassandra's hands urged Kirk to love her. When she felt his heated yet gentle entrance, she cried out his name and they became one again, giving each other the full measure of their love.

They moved together, their hearts and bodies blending into one and carrying each other to the farthest heights of sensation until at last they exploded in a shattering, magnificent climax of love and fulfillment.

When their breathing eased and their minds returned to reality, Cassandra held Kirk a prisoner within her body while she kissed him softly over and over again until finally she relinquished her hold on him and let him come to rest next to her and fitted herself within the sanctuary of his arms.

A few moments later Cassandra realized that he was gazing down at her. "What?" she asked.

"I love looking at you."

"Thank you. . . . Kirk?" she asked, her voice catching when she spoke his name.

"Yes?" he said, instantly alerted by the tone of her voice.

"The year will be over soon."

"I know."

"When it is, can we stop hiding? Can we let the world know how we feel?" As she asked the question that had been in her mind for longer than she cared to admit, her stomach tightened nervously.

Kirk sat up and rested against the headboard. He lifted Cassandra as if she were weightless and turned her so that she faced him while she lay diagonally across his chest.

"You told me a long time ago that when you gave your word, you kept it. Isn't that so?"

"Yes," she agreed, wondering what he was leading up to.

"If we don't make a profit, will you still marry Somner Barwell?"

Cassandra held her breath. Nine months ago the answer would have been easy. Not today. "Kirk, we have to make a profit. We have to!"

"If you had lied to me, I . . ." Kirk began, hating himself for telling the truth.

"I can't lie to you," Cassandra whispered truthfully. Then she blinked and smiled. "Besides, we're already into the black."

"For now. Have the new prices for beef come in?" he asked, his voice changing again.

"Today," Cassandra said with a nod. "But I didn't like them. I'm checking with two other distributors."

Kirk shook his head. "You can't."

"Why? It's our beef; we can sell to whomever we want."

"No, we can't. The Twin Rivers Corporation, under the direction of Leeds International, signed an exclusive distribution agreement with Carway Meat Distributors. It's a four-year contract. This is the second year."

"I didn't realize that," Cassandra said in a distant voice. "I thought we dealt with them because they gave us the best price. Why an exclusive contract?"

"You'll have to ask the home office. It was their decision."

Cassandra sat up, ignoring her nakedness as her thoughts turned exclusively to business. "That's ridiculous. Why would they limit themselves to a single distributor? Especially one who's paying almost fifteen cents a pound under market price. That's unfair."

"Tell me about it," Kirk said sarcastically. "But it's not unheard of, either. Except for the fact that a guaranteed sale makes the exclusive contract desirable." Kirk paused to regroup his thoughts. "Cassandra, I told you once that I thought something wasn't right here."

Cassandra's voice still sounded far away. "It seems almost as if Leeds International doesn't want a profit at Twin Rivers."

"I know."

She closed her eyes for a moment while she tried to grasp at an elusive thought. "It's Father's fail-safe, Kirk. It's what he's counting on to beat us; I know it." Then she shook her head angrily. "There will be a profit. There will be!"

Kirk gazed at Cassandra for a long time afterward, realizing and accepting both the love and the vehemence behind her declaration. Finally, knowing that no words would help, he bent and kissed her deeply before he slid down onto the bed and drew her into his arms.

At seven thirty, Cassandra was at her desk, her fingers flying over the computer keyboard as she drew up file after file, searching for some way to defeat her father. There had to be a way because no matter how much she argued and fought with her father, she loved him and knew that somewhere, buried deep within his own heart, Gregory Leeds loved her and would not lie to her.

But the harder she searched the less certain her convictions became. She was coming to the alarming conclusion that there were too many dealings that did not make sense, too many pieces of a puzzle that did not fit together.

Earlier she had read the original contract between Twin Rivers and the meat distributor and found it completely legal and binding. What she didn't understand was why Leeds International had approved the deal, especially in light of the most important clause of the contract, which dealt with price-setting.

In the contract, Carway Distributors had the right to set beef prices, period! It just didn't make any sense to her. Her father and Murray Charter, who both had to approve any contract, would never have agreed to that clause.

But they had, Cassandra concluded as she glanced at the signatures on the contract and saw her father's bold scrawl on one line and Murray Charter's stodgy penmanship on the other.

By the end of the day, Cassandra knew that she would have to return to New York and confront her father. She would have to face him in person and see his expression when she asked him why they were dealing exclusively with one distributor, to the detriment of the company.

She was deciding whether to tell Kirk or not when her office door opened and he walked in, a worried frown on his handsome face.

"Trouble?" Cassandra asked as he sat down.

"Maybe. One of the men found two of the foals dead, ripped apart."

Cassandra's stomach went queasy with the image that Kirk's words evoked. "What happened?"

"Seems to be a mountain lion. It's unusual, but it happens. We caught one two years ago. That one went for the cattle."

"What can we do?"

"Catch the cat before it kills any more of the horses."

"How?"

"Go after it; hunt the cat down."

"Kill it?" Cassandra asked.

"I hope not," Kirk said in a low voice. "There's usually a reason why a cat goes after livestock. It may be injured."

"Who's going?" she asked, already knowing the answer. "You?"

Kirk nodded. "And a few of the men. I just wanted you to know that I'll be gone for as long as it takes, hopefully only a day or two."

"When are you leaving?"

"Now," he said as he stood.

Cassandra stood, too, and went around her desk and into his already open arms. "Be careful, Kirk, please."

Gazing down at her, Kirk nodded, his mouth set in serious lines. "I will, for you." Then he kissed her, gently, lovingly, and with the promise of many, many more.

After he'd gone, Cassandra sat at her desk for another hour, wondering if she really should go to New York. She glanced at the projections for the sale of the cattle and saw that no matter how she played with the figures, there was no way to make a profit. She had to go to New York.

The only problem she faced would be with Kirk. When he learned she'd gone to New York to challenge her father and demand an explanation about Carway, he would be furious. His pride would get in the way of their happiness. His pride and her father's deceptions could prove the undoing of their love. She couldn't let that happen.

Glancing at her watch, Cassandra saw it was almost six. She stood, stretched, and then left the already deserted offices. She walked past Thelma's desk without stopping to check the stack of messages sitting there, as was her habit. She never saw the pink slip with her name on it and the note that Somner Barwell had called.

She went to the small house where Jane lived and knocked on her door. A moment later it opened, and Jane smiled at her as she dried her red hair. "Hi. Coming for dinner?" she asked. For the last five months, two or three times a week, she and Jane went to the dining hall together for dinner. It had become a ritual she enjoyed.

"Not tonight. Jane, you know about the cougar?"

"Uh-huh," she said, grimacing with disgust. "I was out there today."

"Kirk said he'll probably be gone for a few days."

"At least. He's got to go into the mountains to look for its lair."

"I have to go to New York," Cassandra said.

Jane looked at her and waited.

"I don't want anyone to know," she added.

Jane still didn't speak.

"Can you cover for me?"

"You mean with Kirk?" Jane asked, her stare penetratingly deep.

Cassandra sighed. "You know, don't you?"

"How could I not? I saw it from the beginning," Jane admitted.

Cassandra smiled. "And I thought we had everyone fooled."

"As far as I know, no one else suspects a thing."

"I wish it didn't have to be that way."

"For Kirk, it does," Jane stated sagely. "If you hadn't come here with a big title, it might have been different, but to most of the men . . . the cowboys, it would look as if Kirk was chasing money and selling out."

"But it's not that way."

"The men like you; they're getting to know you. When the time is right, it won't matter to them. But right now it may."

"You really do believe that. You accept it, too, don't you?" Cassandra asked, surprised by this new revelation.

"I accept it because there's no choice. Everything is changing in the world; here it just takes longer. I accept it, yes, but I don't like it. Just remember one thing, Cassandra, both of us—you and I—are living in a man's world."

"So I've noticed," she said dryly.

"Which doesn't mean we can't do what we want." Then Jane took a deep breath. "I know it's none of my business, but . . ."

Cassandra waited, but she saw that Jane was still hesitating. "We're friends, remember?"

"I remember. . . . This trip to New York that you don't want anyone to know about it; is it personal?"

Cassandra smiled broadly. "Business, all business."

"Then why not tell Kirk?"

"Because he wouldn't agree with what I'm going to do.

His pride would get in the way. But I'll tell him when I get back. Will you cover for me?''

"I'll do what I can."

Cassandra had missed the last direct flight to New York, but she'd caught a flight to Dallas and from there by sheer strength of her determination and desire had managed to make all the connecting flights to New York.

At ten o'clock on the morning after her conversation with Jane, she walked into the offices of Leeds International and went straight to her father's private office, only to find him gone.

"When will he be back?" she asked his secretary, Elizabeth.

"He's in Switzerland and isn't expected back for another week. Your mother's with him, too."

"That's surprising," Cassandra commented.

"Not really; it's their anniversary," Elizabeth informed her.

Cassandra closed her eyes and shook her head. "And I'm stupid. Is the office I was using still free?"

"Yes."

"Good. They're staying at the Mont Royal?" Her father's secretary nodded her head. "Elizabeth, could you do a favor for me, please. Would you get me an international florist?"

"Of course," Elizabeth said, her tone softer now.

"Could you also call Mr. Charter. I need to meet with him."

"He's out of town also. He won't be back for two more days."

"I see," Cassandra said. "Okay, I guess I should have

called before I flew back.'' Saying that, Cassandra went to the available office and sat down at the desk. While she waited for the call to the florist, she played absently with the computer.

A moment later the phone rang, and she ordered a large bouquet of flowers, charging them to the company and making a mental note to leave a check with Elizabeth to pay for them when the bill came in. Since her father had canceled her credit cards, Cassandra hadn't bothered to apply for more.

Then Cassandra, refusing to accept the fact that her efforts in traveling to New York had been wasted, began to bring up files from the company's main computer.

Slowly she realized that perhaps this trip had not been futile. She was here, and her father and the comptroller were not. It was a golden opportunity to do some unsuspected checking-up.

Her first order of business was to learn about the Carway contract. Because of the sophistication of the Leeds computer, all the information regarding its subsidiaries was permanently stored in the large mainframe computer. Cassandra had been taught to use the computer during her first week of work, before she'd left for Arizona. What she did now was to request the files for the Twin Rivers Corporation, which was accomplished with a few simple keystrokes on the computer console. Once she had the directory of Twin Rivers on the screen, she looked it over, and called up the contracts file.

Reading it carefully, Cassandra saw that there was no new information, but just as she was about to get the directory back, she noticed a cross-reference notation for Carway Distributors.

Marking down the data base code, Cassandra quickly cleared the screen and called up the new file. When she read the first two lines, her breath exploded.

"So that's your secret," she whispered as she continued to read about Carway Distributors, a wholly owned but well-hidden subsidiary of Leeds International.

Now she knew why the noncompetitive price-setting exclusivity clause had been in the contract. Her father couldn't lose. The lower the price Carway paid for the beef, the higher the profit for Carway.

But why make one part of the company have a deficit to make another show a profit?

Nodding to herself, Cassandra pulled up the profit and loss statements for Carway. She saw that Carway was indeed a big profit maker, much bigger than Twin Rivers would be for several years.

Switching back to the Twin Rivers file, she looked up the tax statements for the last two years. As she suspected, the losses more than balanced out the taxes on Carway. In fact, the losses made up for all the taxes paid by Carway.

Intuitively, though, Cassandra sensed that there was still something that wasn't right. Again Cassandra checked over the directory for Twin Rivers, her eyes speeding from line to line. At the end of the file she paused, backing up the screen as she did.

She studied every entry, until she noted one item that didn't ring true—the land survey file. It had a subfile titled "Geological Findings."

What geological findings? Cassandra asked herself while her fingers pressed the keys that would call up the file.

The screen went blank for a moment, and then letters began to appear. After the fourth line, the cursor blinked maddeningly as it waited for instructions.

"What kind of a geological survey?" she asked aloud as she reread the screen.

GEOLOGICAL SURVEY FINDINGS—TWIN RIVERS
CORPORATION
WARNING! SECURITY CLEARANCE REQUIRED
SECURITY LEVEL 5.0
PLEASE ENTER USER PASSWORD

What is a 5.0 clearance? she wondered. And wondered, too, at the need for a security password. Shrugging her shoulders, Cassandra typed in a random word. The computer responded with quickly formed letters.

ACCESS DENIED—ILLEGAL PASSWORD

"Okay," Cassandra said to the screen. She cleared the screen and stood. Only then did she realize how stiff she was and glanced at her watch. It was almost four o'clock.

Leaving the office, Cassandra crossed the hall and went into the computer department, where she spoke with the data processing supervisor, Mr. Holt.

When she asked about the security clearance level, he gave her a funny look. "I would think you knew about that."

Cassandra shook her head. "I seem not to know about a lot of things around here."

The man didn't think her comment overly funny, and his face attested to that fact. "Most major corporations use a complicated series of security passwords to protect vital information. We have five levels of security here, Miss Leeds. I myself have a 4.0 clearance."

"Who has a 5.0?" she asked.

"Your father and Mr. Charter."

Cassandra smiled in defeat. "I should have known. But why would only one file have security protection?"

"Usually it's because there's confidential information contained in it that must be denied to the casual user."

"I'm far from a casual user," she stated imperiously.

"I'm afraid that anyone not cleared to access the file is a casual user, Miss Leeds," he replied, turning back to his own console in dismissal.

Cassandra left the computer center and went back to the office. She sat before the computer once again and called up the information. Once again she studied the information on the screen and then decided to print it out and take it back to Arizona. Kirk's personnel file had clearly stated his experience with computers operated by the CIA in Vietnam.

She called the airlines and learned that the last direct flight to Phoenix had just departed. If she would like, the airlines informed her, she could take a flight with two stopovers that would get her to Phoenix by five in the morning.

Cassandra, tired from the hectic pace of the past twenty-four hours, decided not to take the flight. Instead she made a reservation on the first direct flight in the morning.

After that, she left the office and went to her parents' town house, where she soaked in a tub for a wonderful hour and then went to bed as the clock struck nine.

Hunting for the mountain lion had been more than just a chore. Although Kirk had three other men with him, being in the mountains and living close to the earth had brought with it a sense of peace and a chance for deep introspection.

The men had seemed to understand Kirk's desire for quiet and for as much privacy as possible. For the two nights and the day they hunted the horse-killer, Kirk barely spoke at all. He'd had too much on his mind to want to make any but the most minimal conversation.

As they had hidden, waiting downwind from the cat's lair for the cougar to return, Kirk was alone with his troubled thoughts.

His last talk with Cassandra still weighed heavily in his thoughts. He had seen in her eyes that if the ranch did not make a profit, he would lose her.

It wasn't right, he told himself. But he also realized that Cassandra was the daughter of one of the world's more powerful men, and as such, her life had never really been her own.

He loved her, he admitted, and loved her so deeply and so passionately that whenever he thought of it, he felt shaken. The reality, too, of time reared its ugly, laughing head. They had six weeks left before the end of the fiscal year.

What can I offer her? he asked himself.

Only my love, he replied silently. He had nothing other than his emotions and his ability to do the work he loved. It would still take another two years before he could afford to buy the ranch he wanted.

It would have been sooner, but in order to go to college after his tour in Vietnam, and in order to make sure that Jane would have a future for herself, he'd had to secure a large loan. It had taken him until three years ago to pay it off.

But Kirk never regretted that. Jane was his only family, and his sense of responsibility ran deep. That she had chosen to return to ranching rather than to pursue a career in psychology made no difference. Her education was important.

What about Cassandra? Kirk had been surprised at how well Cassandra adapted to life on the ranch, but at the same time, he couldn't help but wonder if it was because she had no choice. She had grown up rich, used to having whatever she desired.

Suddenly he heard a low whistle. Instantly alert, Kirk watched the trail leading to the mouth of the lair, which was hidden within a rocky crevice and lit by the newly arriving day.

A moment later he saw the cat. It was a female, sleek and beautiful except for the way she dragged her front leg, which was matted with blood.

Behind him, he heard one of the men cock his rifle. Quickly he raised his hand to stop him. The cat was too beautiful to destroy if it could be saved. Turning, Kirk reached into the small pack and withdrew a long cylindrical object. As the cat neared the lair Kirk picked up his rifle and loaded it with the tranquilizer dart.

Raising the rifle, he centered the sight on the cat's flank and, without hesitating, pulled the trigger. The dart struck the cougar and she whirled, snarling at her unseen enemy. In less than fifteen seconds, the cat had fallen helplessly to the ground.

Kirk and the three hands rose from their concealment and walked over to the cat. None of the men spoke; each of them held his rifle, eyes wary. But the cat did not move; its large golden eyes were open but empty.

"Jeez, look at that paw," one of the men said after he was certain that the cat would not move.

The men studied the paw, and Kirk, sure that the drug would sedate the cat for a good six hours, bent close to it.

"At least we know why it was going after the horses."

"What do you think happened?" asked another.

Kirk lifted the injured leg and grimaced. "Stepped in a trap. I don't know how the hell she got out." Then he stood. "Let's get her tied up and over to the Rover. We'll bring her to the vet and let him figure out what to do."

"She'll never be able to hunt again," commented one of the hands.

"Maybe a zoo will take her," Kirk replied.

The men worked quickly and efficiently, and an hour and a half later, the cat, suspended between two very nervous horses, was brought out of the mountains.

After the cat was secured in the back of the Land-Rover, Kirk picked one of the men to accompany him to the vet while the other two men returned to the ranch.

Although the hunt was over, Kirk should have been happy with the way things had ended, but he wasn't. In fact, he felt somewhat akin to the cougar—tied on a limb and unsure of when he'd be released, if ever.

The one thing he did know was that when he got back to the ranch, he would have a talk with Cassandra—a very serious talk. He was no longer willing to play this game that she and her father were involved in.

Cassandra would have to make up her mind, one way or the other. It was either Cassandra and Kirk, or Cassandra and her money. Kirk refused to accept the fact that his emotions were being staked on a profit and loss statement.

Chapter Fourteen

$\mathcal{K}$irk pulled up to the main house, shut off the engine, and climbed out of the Rover. His timing couldn't have been better: the office staff would be eating lunch in the dining hall and Cassandra, he hoped, would be alone.

The moment he'd dropped the cougar off, he'd driven straight back to the ranch, his mind set purposefully on the confrontation with Cassandra that could wait no longer. The long hours spent deep in thought had set his mind on a single purpose. Kirk had to know what was happening with his life: he had to know the truth about Cassandra's feelings.

He had watched her change dramatically over the past eleven months. He loved and wanted her but did not know if she would be willing to give up everything that had been hers all her life.

Taking long bold strides, Kirk entered the house and

went straight into Cassandra's office. But when he looked around, he saw she was not there.

Jane had told him that she'd gone to Phoenix yesterday because of some banking problems, but he'd fully expected to see her today. *Maybe she's at the dining hall,* he thought. But as he started to turn he glanced at her desk and saw the stack of messages sitting on it.

That wasn't at all like Cassandra. She had always been extremely efficient about answering her messages. But the large stack denied that fact.

Walking to the desk, Kirk glanced at the top memo. It was from the Blackstone Dude Ranch, inquiring about a horse. It was dated yesterday, at three P.M.

Cassandra would never hold off on something like that—it meant profits. Sensing something was wrong, Kirk leafed through the stack of messages until one caught his eye.

His muscles tensed, and his blood ran cold when he read the name. Somner Barwell. The message was dated two days ago, the same day he'd left to go after the cat. The message was simple: CALL ME SOON. IMPORTANT.

"What's important?" he asked, suddenly suspicious and angry. He knew he had no reason to be angry, but as he put the messages down he couldn't squelch this new uneasy feeling. The message was a reminder to Kirk of just how tenuous he felt his hold on Cassandra was.

Kirk left the offices and walked across to the dining hall, hoping to find Cassandra there and to find out also why Somner Barwell was calling her. But even as he thought of this, he paused.

Slow down, he ordered himself. *Barwell was a part of her life before Twin Rivers. She can talk to whomever she wants*. Trying to make himself accept that, he went into the dining hall. A moment later he saw she wasn't there. But he saw Jane off to one side and joined her at the table.

"Hey, boss man, welcome home. Catch your cat?" she asked with a smile.

"She's at Doc Mason's," he said. "Hasn't Cassandra gotten back from Phoenix yet?"

Jane took a sip of coffee as she decided how to answer him. "I haven't seen her today," she replied truthfully. "Tell me about the cat."

Kirk was about to beg off, but instead he took a deep breath and nodded. "She's a beauty," he began.

Cassandra returned to Arizona and Twin Rivers, and as soon as she stepped out of the Land-Rover, she knew she had returned home. Under the heat of the midday sun, she realized that she had not enjoyed her time in New York. She'd disliked the grayness, the chilly air, and the frowning, tense faces that had surrounded her.

Shaking her head at this new discovery, Cassandra walked into the house and up to her suite. She was glad to be back and anxious to tell Kirk about the things she'd learned. She'd done a lot of thinking on the plane, trying to figure a way out of the sinister trap her father had conjured.

In the apartment, Cassandra unpacked her small bag before changing out of one of the two designer dresses she'd worn on the trip. Then she changed into a pair of jeans, a top, and her now well-broken-in boots. Twenty-five minutes after arriving at the ranch, Cassandra went into her office, just as Thelma returned from lunch.

"Thelma," Cassandra called. "Has Kirk gotten back yet?"

"He just got back. He's at the dining hall," Thelma informed her.

"Thank you," Cassandra said as she went into her office, where she saw the large stack of waiting messages. When she neared the bottom of the pile, she found the message from Somner, marked important.

Staring at it brought back the memory of that long-ago day and the unsuspected anger that had come over him. "Nothing's that important," she said, balling up the note and throwing it in the trash can.

Sitting back, Cassandra closed her eyes and thought of how different she was from the woman who had dined with Somner eleven months before.

She was so lost in her thoughts she didn't hear the footsteps approaching her desk. Yet she sensed that someone was staring at her.

Opening her eyes, she found Kirk gazing down at her. "Hi," she said in a throaty voice. A warm feeling spread through her at the sight of his handsome face. "Did you have good hunting?"

Kirk gazed at her for a few seconds. "I would have rather had no hunting at all. How are you?"

"Good, Kirk, now . . ." she said honestly. Then she sat straighter in the chair. She wanted to go to him, to be held within his strong arms, but she saw the office door was open. Instead she spoke to him. "Kirk, I may have found out what my father's plan is."

Kirk remained silent and waited for her to continue.

Standing, Cassandra went to the door and closed it. When she turned back to face Kirk, she saw he was scrutinizing her intently.

Kirk drank in her beauty, amazed that after all this time,

she looked even more beautiful than when he'd first seen her. He wanted to talk to her, to find out once and for all what their future would be. But he held himself back.

"I was in New York yesterday," she began. When she saw the surprised look on his face, she raced on. "I flew out when you went after the cat. I just got back."

Kirk's gaze hardened, but she didn't notice it as she went on. "I went there to talk to my father."

"And?" The single word was loud and harsh, but he didn't care.

"He wasn't there; neither was Mr. Charter. So I decided to take the opportunity to use the computer, and I found out why we sell our cattle only to Carway Distributors." Cassandra paused to take a breath and to study Kirk's face, which had grown very tense while she'd spoken.

"Leeds International owns Carway Distributors. The reason the price is so low is that Twin Rivers' losses offset the Carway profits. Taxwise, Leeds actually makes more aftertax profit."

Kirk nodded. "Your father's a devious man."

"He's also a good businessman. What he's doing makes sense in the overall picture for Leeds International."

"And Twin Rivers is only a small cog in a big wheel," Kirk stated as more of the pieces of the elusive puzzle fell into place.

Kirk couldn't think logically, however. He was still hearing her say that she had gone to New York; he was remembering the message from Somner Barwell, dated the same day she'd flown out. Jane had told him she was in Phoenix. *Why the lie?*

"There's more," Cassandra said.

"What else could there be? Your father's taken care of everything."

Misinterpreting the angry tones in Kirk's voice, Cassandra went to her desk and picked up the computer printout. "You never talk about your past, never," she began when she was facing him again. "Not about growing up, not about the time you were in the army. You were in intelligence, weren't you?"

"You read my personnel file," he stated flatly.

"Yes. Kirk . . . why would Father have had a geological survey done on Twin Rivers?"

Kirk's brow wrinkled, caught off guard by Cassandra's twisting conversation. "Just routine—no real reason."

"There has to be one. Father doesn't do anything without a reason," she stated as she handed him the sheet of paper. "I found that in one of the files."

Kirk looked at the paper and then at Cassandra. "And?"

"It means something, Kirk. It's important, and I think it has something to do with what's going on here."

"What do you want me to do about it?"

"I don't know. When I remembered that you were in military intelligence in Vietnam, I thought maybe you could figure out the password and we could find out what the geological survey was for."

Kirk shook his head. "Cassandra, you need an expert to break into a computer security system. It could take years to work out the password. That wasn't my specialty. Besides," he said with a shrug, "what difference will it make now? Your father's won—Carway was the deciding factor."

Cassandra stared at him in disbelief. "What are you saying?"

"Haven't you figured it out yet? You came up with a way to show a profit. You almost beat your father by using future sales on the horses. But your father came up with a way to defeat the profits by having Carway lower the price for the cattle. And, as you said, you 'never break your promises.' When is the wedding?''

Cassandra shook her head violently, denying his words with every beat of her heart. ''There has to be a way,'' she whispered as the truth of his words struck with the sharpness of a knife.

''I thought we were working together,'' Kirk said suddenly, unable to stop himself from venting his bitterness.

Cassandra, taken aback by the angry tone in his voice, replied hesitantly. ''We are.''

''Are we? Why did you lie to Jane about going to Phoenix when you actually went to New York?'' With that question, Kirk knew he had drawn the battle lines.

Cassandra's anger caused her to think irrationally. She was bone tired, and everything she'd learned in the past two days had dulled her usually sharp perceptions. Her father's deception had saddened her, and the possible defeat at his hands hurt her deeply. Kirk's tone, along with his accusatory glare, were the final straws.

''What I did, I did for us! I don't know what happened while I was gone, but you have no right to say those things. I went to New York to find answers. Answers that you've been looking for!'' With that, Cassandra took a deep breath and stared at Kirk's tight features.

Intuitively she knew that it was not her trip to New York that bothered Kirk—it was something else.

''What, Kirk? What are you trying to say?''

Kirk shook his head. He almost laughed aloud, but he didn't. He had come here to talk to her. To ask her to spend her life with him on a ranch. But now he knew better. He had finally come to the realization that his hopes for the future were nothing more than pointless fantasies; Cassandra Leeds was indeed a different breed than he.

"The game's over. For a while I thought I had a chance; for a while I believed it. But I see how wrong I was. Cassandra, those silken threads that attach you to your father are too strong for you to break." With that, Kirk walked stiffly past her and reached for the doorknob, the computer printout clutched, forgotten, in his hand.

"Kirk," Cassandra whispered.

Kirk stopped, his shoulders stiff. He turned only his head.

"Don't shut me out again! Stay and talk to me."

"I don't think I will this time," he said as he opened the door and left.

Behind him, staring helplessly at his retreating back, Cassandra drooped, her numbed mind refusing to accept what had just happened.

Cassandra pulled back on Suzi's reins just as she crested the low rise. When the horse stopped, Cassandra turned in the saddle to look at the golden-hued glory surrounding her. Next to her, Jane Paulson did the same.

As Cassandra gazed at the sunset she thought about the two weeks that had followed the strange scene in her office. Each day since Kirk had walked out of the office had passed with the speed of a century. For Cassandra, each day was endless.

But her nights were the worst—dark and sleepless hours caused by her inability to understand what had happened between her and Kirk.

She had tried to speak to him several times, but whenever she mentioned anything about the two of them, he'd stop her cold, refusing to discuss anything but business.

"Ready to talk yet?" Jane asked as she studied Cassandra's face.

"Talk?" Cassandra asked innocently.

Jane laughed. "If I didn't know better, I'd think you grew up out here. Silent cowboy and all that stuff. Come on, Cassandra, you haven't been yourself for weeks. What happened?"

"It doesn't matter," she whispered.

"Of course not. That's why you've kept yourself locked up in the main house since you got back from New York."

"Jane . . ."

"No, ma'am, I remember when you first got here. You were a frightened woman, pretending you weren't. You pretended so well that you ended up making everyone at Twin Rivers dislike you. But you were strong enough to change all that. Why revert now?"

"Why not?" she asked bitterly. "What difference does anything make anymore?"

"You mean you're giving up?" Jane asked harshly.

Cassandra stared at her, her mind unaffected by her friend's words. "If you want to call it that. Or maybe someone gave up on me."

Grasping the reins tightly, Cassandra started to turn Suzi. Jane, seeing this, reached out and stopped her. "Wait!"

"Jane—"

"Cassandra, I thought we were friends?"

"We are."

"Are we? Do you always turn your back on your friends?"

"I . . ." Cassandra began but stopped. She looked into Jane's eyes, and suddenly the wall she had erected around herself tumbled. Words poured from her as she told Jane the story of her father's deception with the meat distribution and of Kirk's sudden rejection. When she was finished, she stared at Jane helplessly.

"There's nothing you can do about your father, but do you remember what you said to me when you left for New York?"

Cassandra shrugged.

"You said you didn't want Kirk to know yet, because of his pride. Isn't that what it's all about?"

Cassandra considered Jane's question, and then slowly shook her head. "I don't think so. I think it's something else. Something he won't discuss."

"Ask him!"

"He won't listen to anything except business."

"Make him," Jane stated. "Make him listen to you!"

"I don't know if I can."

"Getting a person to listen to you is easy. Getting him to hear you is the hard part," Jane said.

"Is that from one of your psychology textbooks?" Cassandra asked.

Jane shook her head. "It's one of my cousin's sayings."

Cassandra smiled. "I really do want to meet him one day."

"You will; I promise you. But talk to Kirk."

"I'll try," Cassandra said, relenting.

The music jarred loudly in Kirk's ears, but he didn't care. He lifted his drink and stared at himself in the barroom mirror. He didn't like what he saw. His eyes had a vacant faraway look in them. His mouth was tight and his jaw was stiff.

During the last weeks he'd become a loner, speaking only when spoken to and answering in monosyllabic replies. He was growing more distant from his work, and from caring what happened at Twin Rivers.

Only once had he thought about the ranch with any real concern, and that had been on the very afternoon Cassandra had given him the computer printout. Not even knowing why he was bothering, late that night he'd called a friend of his, a man he'd worked with in 'Nam. Darren Hawks had been a computer expert in army intelligence during the war. As a civilian, he worked with the State Department.

When Kirk had reached him, he'd explained what he'd found and asked if there was a way to break into the system to find the password. Darren had been noncommittal but had promised to look into it.

"I haven't seen you drinking alone since—" Jane's voice interrupted his thoughts.

"You were twelve," Kirk finished for her.

"Fourteen actually. You came home on leave."

"What?"

"Can we talk?"

"Are you asking if I'm sober?"

"Can we talk?" Jane reiterated.

Kirk nodded his head. "Go on."

"Why are you treating her this way?"

"Why not? I got seduced into playing rich people's games for stakes that are too high."

"Are they?"

"They were."

"You're in love with her," Jane stated with finality.

"So what? She'll be marrying the very rich Somner Barwell after the end of the fiscal year."

"If you let her."

"Wrong. It's her . . . game."

"I don't think it is a game. I think you're making it into one so that your own bruised ego can survive."

Kirk turned and stared at Jane, his eyes hard and flat. "Don't give me a lecture about myself," he warned, his voice a low growl.

"Don't try to scare me. I'm not ten years old anymore. Kirk, Cassandra loves you. She's terribly hurt by whatever it is you've done to her."

"Me? I think you've got things backward."

"Do I, Kirk? Do I really?"

"Really!" Kirk said tersely.

Jane gazed at her cousin, the man she respected and loved above any other person in the world, and found herself unable to accept the changes she saw in him.

"I grew up having you set examples for me. You taught me how to love, how to feel, and how to be a person. When I lost my self-confidence, you showed me how to get it back. I want to do that for you, but I don't know if I can. You also taught me never to quit, never to run away. What happened to you, Kirk?"

"I realized my limitations," he answered in a barely audible whisper.

Jane stood slowly. Her hand went to his shoulder and squeezed it. "No, Kirk, you just narrowed them."

When Jane was gone, Kirk stared at the drink. He lifted it, but before it reached his lips, he'd set it down.

A moment later he was out of the bar and behind the wheel of the Land-Rover. An hour and a half later he pulled the vehicle off the road and cut across the moonlit terrain until he reached a spot he hadn't returned to in the last eighteen years.

There, under the gentle glow of the moon, he looked around at the land that had once been his, and remembered who he was and where he'd come from, and remembered, too, the promises he had made long ago.

The sun was up when Kirk returned to his house. As he walked to the bedroom he'd seen the red flashes blinking on his answering machine. He rewound the tape and played the messages back. The first was from Cliff Showmen, reporting a break in the north border fence. The second was from Darren Hawks in Washington.

Looking at his watch, Kirk saw that it was only five o'clock in Washington and he would have to wait before calling Darren. To kill the time, he took a shower, dressed in fresh clothing, and drove to the northern border to check the fencing. He found that the damage was minimal, but the fencing was old, and at least a half a mile of it would have to be replaced.

When he returned, the hands were getting ready to start working. He found Cliff Showmen and told him to get the fence repaired immediately, because they would be driving the herd there in two days.

Although Kirk wasn't hungry, he went inside and ate a small breakfast. When he was done, he returned to his house and called Washington. Ten minutes later he hung up the phone, a shadowy smile on his face.

Darren Hawks had somehow found a way to bypass the security of the Leeds computer. When Kirk had asked him how, Darren's voice had changed, warning Kirk not to ask any more questions. "Let's just say that we have our ways."

Kirk sat back and smiled to himself. He opened his desk drawer, took out the small leather pouch, and rolled a very rare cigarette. After it was lit, he took a deep draw and let the smoke fill the air.

There had been many things that he'd wanted to find out about the Leeds corporation. If nothing else, before he packed his bags and left, at least he would get some answers.

At two o'clock, Cassandra stood, gazing out the office window, wondering how she should approach Kirk. After talking with Jane, she'd realized that because of his own foolish pride, Kirk would never make up to her. If anything was to come of their relationship, it must be she who took the initiative.

Cassandra knew that if she wanted a life with Kirk, she couldn't wait any longer. She had to talk to him; they had to figure out a way to beat her father in the two weeks that remained. She loved him too much to let a stupid, irrational promise, given out of desperation, destroy the rest of her life.

Tonight! she declared.

Even as she made up her mind, the drone of a low-flying plane cut through the silence of the office as it descended onto the airstrip.

"Who?" she asked aloud, waiting at the window for several minutes until she saw a lone figure walking toward the house. Her breath caught when she recognized Somner Barwell.

Now what? she asked herself. She thought about going out to meet him but decided against it and returned to the desk, spreading out several pages to make herself look busy.

A few minutes later Thelma stepped into her office and announced, "a Mr. Barwell to see you."

"Send him in," Cassandra said, lifting the papers and stacking them as Somner walked into the office.

"Cassie," he said in a loud voice as he went around the desk and bent to kiss her.

Cassandra turned her face, giving Somner her cheek. "This is a surprise," she said in cool tones.

"I had to see you," he informed her as he walked back around the desk and sat in one of the two chairs. "My, you do appear to be extremely efficient."

"Thank you. Why did you have to see me?" she asked.

"You look lovely in your cowgirl outfit," he said with a wide smile. "You seem to have made yourself fit in nicely."

"Why are you here, Somner?" she repeated.

"Cassie, stop being so cold. I'm here for two reasons. The first is to apologize for the way I acted that day."

"You'll never be able to apologize for that," Cassandra stated, unable to hide the anger in her voice. At the same time, Cassandra steeled herself to face him and maintain her own convictions, no matter what.

"I hope I will," he said, unperturbed by her words. "You see, the second reason I'm here is to give you good news," he said with a proud look on his self-satisfied features.

"Yes?" she asked when his pause lengthened into an uncomfortable silence.

"I've done a lot of thinking since we had our . . . ah . . . little disagreement last spring. I acted foolishly, without thinking. Cassandra, I do love you, and I want to marry you. We make a perfect couple. We complement each other, and we're good for each other."

"Is that your good news?"

Somner didn't seem to hear the sarcasm in her reply or if

he did, he was ignoring it. "No, just the prelude. Father is partially retiring. I am being named president of Barwell Industries. Before that happens, Father insists that I spend the next six months running our European division so that I will be totally familiar with all aspects of our companies."

"Congratulations, Somner," Cassandra said in an even voice.

"I must leave in two days. Cassandra, come with me. We'll be married in Paris and honeymoon in Nice. I know how you love Nice. Afterward we'll work together. You can take any job you want. Anything you desire."

Cassandra leaned back in her chair and studied Somner for several long minutes before she shook her head. "No, Somner, I won't marry you."

"Why?" he asked, bewildered at this latest refusal. "I apologized for my actions in New York. Cassie, that will never happen again."

"I know. The truth is that I don't love you. And I won't be possessed by any man! Good-bye," she said in a voice edged with steel.

Somner shook his head slowly. "Cassie, I think the sun out here has addled your brains. You don't belong here, with cows and horses and hay. You belong with me. Don't you understand what I'm offering you?"

Cassandra didn't let her anger rule her words; instead she nodded her head to him. "Only too well."

This time Somner's eyes hardened, and his features grew taut. "I won't ask you again," he stated.

"Thank you for that!"

Somner looked at her for several long seconds. "You're making a mistake you'll regret for the rest of your life."

"No, I'm making a decision that will give me back the rest of my life. Good-bye, Somner."

Somner glared at her until finally he stood. "You're a silly fool," he snapped, turning and walking out of the office in quick, curiously ungraceful strides.

"A fool maybe," she whispered, "but not stupid." Cassandra realized that her anger was not provoked by Somner's brazen gall in showing up eleven-and-a-half months after their last meeting to apologize for the way he'd acted. She was sure it had not been coincidence that had brought him here.

Until the very second Cassandra had spoken her final words to him, she hadn't realized that she had made up her mind.

It was more than Somner's appearance that had spurred Cassandra to her decision; he had only been a catalyst. She had finally seen the futility of her attempts to save Twin Rivers, and she knew it no longer made a difference. Win or lose, she would not be returning to her father's domination. She was no longer a pawn in his business machinations. The game was over, and with it had gone her innocence.

Standing, Cassandra tried to control her emotions as she went to the door to watch Somner leave the outer office and her life.

Chapter Fifteen

In a corner of the main office, Kirk sat, half hidden by a computer console, his fingers racing over the keys.

He had chosen this time—noon in New York—because most of the data personnel at Leeds would be out to lunch, which meant there would be less chance of them detecting an outside source that was looking into the computer memory banks via the telephone modem.

As he entered the string of passwords, one by one, that Darren Hawks had given him, he glanced up to see a well-remembered face standing at Thelma's desk—Somner Barwell's.

His body tensed. A moment later when Somner went into Cassandra's office, Kirk's anger flared anew.

Last night he had wondered if he had indeed lost his self-confidence. Before he'd arrived back at his house and found the message from Darren, he'd decided he would speak to Cassandra and tell her how he felt, regardless of the consequences. He had to do it for his own peace of mind.

Now, with the appearance of Somner Barwell, Kirk realized that once again words were to no avail. Cassandra's year was almost over, and Barwell had come to claim his prize. He punched the keys angrily as he entered the next password. An instant later the computer screen was filled with data and charts. When he finished reading, he lifted his eyes from the screen, his mind strangely calm. *Bastard!*

As he cursed Gregory Leeds he saw Cassandra's office door open and Somner Barwell walk stiffly away, his face set in angry lines. A moment later Cassandra appeared in the office doorway, a sad but determined look on her face for the few seconds she remained there.

After she was gone, Kirk went back to the console and checked one last detail at Leeds International. When he was finished, he stood and went to Cassandra's office. It took him ten long strides to reach her door and step inside, where he saw her staring out the window.

"Cassandra," he called. She turned to him, and he saw her eyes were filled with tears. "We have to talk."

Cassandra felt as if she were mired in the thickest mud. She gazed at Kirk, and let the feelings of her love for him surface for one pitying moment before she dismissed them, turning her thoughts to business.

"Talk about what?" she asked, taking a deep breath.

"About Leeds International."

"Why? It's over, Kirk. We've wasted a year beating a dead horse."

Kirk ignored the strain in her voice. "Don't you want to know what's going on? I found out about the geological survey, and I can guess about all the rest."

Cassandra shrugged her shoulders. "My father lied to

me, Kirk. He made a deal with me, let me think I had a chance, and then extracted a promise from me for what *he* wanted. But he lied to get it.''

"That's big business, isn't it? Isn't that what you told me?'' Kirk challenged.

"Yes,'' she admitted, "but I believed I could do it! I really did.''

"It's all academic now whether you made a profit or not. You see, the ranch was never ever intended to make money.''

"Why? Just to let Carway earn a few extra profit dollars?''

"Do you really want to know what it's all about—this game your father's playing with Twin Rivers?''

"He's playing it with me, and with you, too, Kirk.''

"Not any longer . . . but that doesn't matter. The geological survey shows that there are vast—and I do mean vast—quantities of natural gas under Twin Rivers. There may be oil, too, but it's the natural gas your father—Leeds International—is after.''

Cassandra stared at him, puzzled. "Then why keep the ranch operating?''

"Two reasons. The first is to make Carway a bigger operation. It makes a lot of sense to build up the profits on the distribution end and to take the tax losses on the breeding. The government has several tax shelter benefits for farm losses, and it looks plausible in the annual shareholders' report.''

Kirk paused for a moment as he searched Cassandra's eyes. It was harder than he'd expected to tell her the news. He loved her, and that hurt, too, knowing that their time together was over.

"The second part is more difficult to explain, because it's

guesswork. Leeds International, according to the computer, has been trying to get into the petrogas market for three years. But it's a hard market to crack unless you're willing to lay out a lot of cash and take gigantic losses for several years. The only other way is to take over a smaller company that doesn't have a lot of reserve fields. That's what your father is doing.''

The facts and figures that Kirk had just learned flashed through his mind with maddening speed. ''Three years ago, Leeds International began buying the stock of the Inter Ocean Exploration Company. Because they didn't want the prices to go too high, they bought only small blocks. As of right now, they own a good portion of stock, but not enough to complete the takeover. According to the Leeds projections, that takeover will occur in the next year and a half.''

''I'm not following you,'' Cassandra admitted, although she had been so lost in what he was saying that the deceptions and heartaches of the past year had fled in their wake.

''You will,'' he said, his voice warmer than he'd intended. ''Once they own the company, Twin Rivers will go out of business and the gas-drilling will start.''

''But why keep it a secret? What difference does it make?''

''Plenty. First of all, Leeds is most likely buying up as much land in the area as it can, knowing how the gas is disbursed. Second, they must fight the environmentalists. To do this, they have to use the ranch as a cover. Only when the drilling is started will anyone know what's happening. By then, the opposition will have an uphill battle to stop it.''

"How can you be so certain?" Cassandra asked, unwilling to believe what she'd heard.

"As I said, it's all conjecture, but it's nothing new. It happens all the time."

"What you're saying is that in two years, Twin Rivers will be just a bunch of natural gas fields?"

"Exactly!"

"They can't! They can't destroy it!" Cassandra cried, turning away from Kirk to look out the window at the beautiful land. Suddenly she saw Somner's plane take off.

"I'm sure he's happy to know he's won you," Kirk said in a low voice.

Cassandra stiffened, her emotions running on a wild rampage, tears filling her eyes. Turning suddenly, she gazed at Kirk through a hazy film of moisture. "Damn you, Kirk North! I'm not a pawn to be played at the whims of everyone but myself."

Kirk stared at her and saw the crystal tears run down her cheeks. His throat tightened; his heart wavered. He took a deep breath. "Cassandra, I came in here to tell you two things: First, I'm not a pawn, either. I'm handing in my resignation today. I'll leave as soon as possible. Second—I love you, and I want to spend the rest of my life with you. But I know how different we are, and I understand how hard it would be for you to give up everything you've always had. I don't have the right to ask that of you."

Cassandra's world spun. At first she had trouble accepting what he was saying, but the way her heart sang told her the truth. She took a deep breath, her eyes sweeping across the planes of his face.

"No, you don't have that right. Only I do."

"And you don't break your promises."

"No, I don't break my promises," she repeated, her voice growing lighter instead of heavier.

Kirk watched the green flashes of fire sparkle in the hazel depths of her eyes and, for no reason at all, his emotions swelled.

"Somner Barwell is a lucky man."

"Somner Barwell is a pompous fool who thinks that money, looks, and parental approval are the most important things in life."

"But a lot more secure than an itinerant cowboy."

Cassandra was silent, her breath trapped in her chest, not because of Kirk's words, but because of a powerful, cutting thought that held her transfixed for an eternal minute. In two days she would be twenty-eight years old, and it had taken her all that time to discover exactly what she wanted out of life. With that knowledge came the release of the shackles that had held her prisoner to her own fears, and to her father.

She let her breath escape, and smiled. "The last thing in the world that anyone could call you is an itinerant cowboy, Kirk North."

"What am I?" he asked, his voice low, his nerves tense.

"The man I love. The man I want to spend my life with, working with, and loving with."

Kirk gazed at her, his hands clenching and unclenching at his sides. "But you have your bargain with your father."

Cassandra nodded her head slowly in agreement with Kirk, yet the challenge was still on her face when she spoke. "I gave my word to my father. We made a bargain, and I kept my part. I accepted his conditions, and I met them. I succeeded—we succeeded—in doing what I set out to do. And we both know that, don't we, Kirk?"

"We know we could have done it."

"Yes, we could have!" Cassandra stated. "If my father had given me an honest chance to prove myself. I gave him my promise in good faith. He broke that faith; he broke the contract between us."

"He played to win," Kirk reminded her in a gentle voice.

"No. What he did was to rig everything so that he could beat me down and make me do what he wanted."

"What about Somner? Wasn't he just here to claim his spoils?"

"He left alone, didn't he?" she asked, her voice harsh. "I told him I would never marry him. I plan on telling my father the same thing. I . . . I want to tell him something else also," Cassandra added.

"What?" Kirk asked, his eyebrows raised, sensing that his destiny was about to be pronounced.

Cassandra, her hands suddenly trembling, locked them together. "About us—about our future." After saying it, she felt as though the weight of the world was pressing down on her heart. She thought she would fall but, bracing her legs, she stood, waiting.

"Do we have one?" Kirk asked in a tight voice.

Cassandra didn't answer right away; she knew her reply was too important to just fling words at him. She closed her eyes for a moment. "When I came here, I didn't know what having a future meant. I knew that I would always have the security of my father's money, his influence, and his position in the world. But a future. . . . ." She shrugged. "I had no idea what that was. Now I do—or I don't. And that, Kirk North, will be up to you to decide."

Hearing the emotion and honesty in her voice was the key

that broke down his last defense. He gazed at her, drinking in her beauty, and made up his mind. "Do you really think you can handle being a cowboy's wife?"

Cassandra, her heart beating out of control, went up to him, slipped her arms around his back, and stared directly into his warm brown eyes. "I thought you'd never ask."

The week that followed Cassandra's confrontation with Kirk passed faster than any other time in her life. She knew how deeply she loved him and was just as sure of his love for her.

She was determined, too, that her father would not stop their marriage. To that end, she and Kirk planned every last detail with excruciating calculation.

In exactly seven days her father would arrive for the final accounting. In seven days, he would get his accounting, and much, much more.

She had asked Kirk not to hand in his resignation yet, but to give it to her father in person. He had agreed, liking the plan she had developed in order to extract the full pleasure of handing her father his defeat in the face of what Gregory Leeds considered to be an accepted victory.

Their only argument had come when they discussed marriage. Kirk wanted to wait until everything was settled with her father, instead of sneaking off to be married in secret.

"But it doesn't make any difference," she'd stated.

"You'll have the rest of your life to look back on our marriage and wonder if we shouldn't have waited," he had advised.

"Are you getting cold feet?" she'd asked jokingly.

"You keep them warm enough," he'd replied with a smile that made her heart beat faster.

"Then what is it?"

"Sneaking off into the night isn't the way to get married. And," he said as his arms tightened around her, "you gave your word to do a job, even if your father did deceive you. You have to see the fiscal year through to its end, if only for your own peace of mind."

Cassandra gazed at him and kissed him, putting all the love she had into the kiss. When it had ended, she drew back. "You're right, Kirk. We'll wait, but not a minute past the appointed hour!"

The three-hundred-and-sixty-fourth day was just ending, and the three-hundred-and-sixty-fifth would arrive with the dawn. For Cassandra, it would be the most important day in her life.

When the sun rose, she would face her father, and she would marry Kirk. It was an exciting day that loomed close for Cassandra—much too exciting to miss out on a single second.

After eating a light dinner with Kirk, she had kissed him good night at her door, and then packed two of the five suitcases she'd arrived with at Twin Rivers. After that, she'd set out the dress she would wear, the dress she and Jane had picked up just that afternoon.

When that was done, she went to bed and tried to sleep, but sleep was elusive. When three o'clock came and went, Cassandra could not stay in bed any longer. She dressed in jeans, a sweatshirt, and a pair of moccasins, and went out for a walk.

An hour later she returned, unable to sleep, still restless and wondering what would happen when she faced her father. But she forced herself to lie down and fell into a light, dreamless sleep.

At seven o'clock, Cassandra took a shower and did her hair. At a quarter to eight, she put on the dress she'd bought yesterday, adjusting it so that its lines fell smoothly. Even as she did, she heard a knock on her door.

She opened it and smiled at Jane.

"I thought you could use some help."

"I need the company more," Cassandra said.

"Nervous?" Jane asked.

"Not about today."

"Then what?"

"Next year, ten years . . ."

"Don't be silly," Jane advised.

"I can't help it, Jane. I've done a lot of things in my life, but I've never done anything quite like this before."

"Are you afraid it won't last?" Jane asked, a frown wrinkling her brow as she reached out and adjusted the right sleeve of Cassandra's dress.

"No. Nothing that simple. It's my father. He's always been ruthless. And I'm afraid that he might take his anger out on Kirk . . . blame Kirk for what's happened."

Jane shook her head slowly. "Kirk's a big boy; don't worry about him. Turn around," she ordered. Cassandra sighed and did as Jane requested. "I love the dress. I'm glad I helped you pick it out," she said as she looked over the simple yet elegantly hand-worked western dress.

"You're sure it's not too . . . much?"

"No, it really is perfect."

"Jane—"

"You know, as my cousin once told me, if you worry too much about the future, the past will be all you have."

"Are you sure your cousin's a rancher and not a philosophy professor? And," Cassandra added quickly before Jane could speak, "when am I going to meet him?"

"Cassandra," Jane began, hesitating as she tried to figure out a way to tell Cassandra just who her cousin was. "I have to—" she began again but was cut off by a loud knock on the door.

"Who?" Cassandra asked.

Jane shrugged. "I'll check," she said and went to the door. She opened it only wide enough to see it was Kirk, wearing a deep-blue western-cut suit. She held up her hand and turned back to Cassandra.

"Who is it?" Cassandra asked.

"Remember that check you offered me a long time ago for teaching you to ride?" When Cassandra nodded, Jane went on. "Are we friends? Really good friends?"

"Of course," Cassandra replied, puzzled.

"Okay," Jane said and took a deep breath. "Cassandra Leeds, I'd like you to meet my cousin—" On the word *cousin*, Jane opened the door.

Cassandra, surprised, became instantly alert. When the door opened, and she saw Kirk standing there, she didn't understand Jane's meaning.

"—my cousin, Kirk North," she finally said.

Cassandra knew her jaw had dropped, but she couldn't help but stare into the smiling faces across from her. "He's your cousin?" she asked, her tone accusatory.

"I wanted to tell you, but I never got the chance."

Cassandra looked from Jane to Kirk, her head shaking slowly. But before she said anything, Kirk stepped forward. "Are you ready?" he asked, his eyes sweeping over her from head to toe.

Cassandra did the same and her breath caught in her throat. He looked so handsome standing before her that her heart ached with love.

"I am now," she whispered, her earlier nervousness gone completely.

A half-hour later Cassandra was standing on the lawn in front of the main house. Her thoughts were tinged with sadness, although she wasn't really sad. "Kirk, I love you, and I want to thank you for being here with me."

Kirk grinned and came up to her. His arms went around her, and his mouth closed on hers. The kiss was a gently warm reassurance that everything would work out right. When they parted, he caressed her cheek.

"I wouldn't have it any other way." To accent his words, the sound of a twin-engine plane reached them. "They're here," he said.

"Everything is ready?" she asked.

"And waiting. Let's go to the office and wait. Jamie is driving them from the airstrip."

Cassandra nodded and, placing her hand in Kirk's, they walked the twenty yards from the small house to the main building, where they both went into her office.

Five minutes later Gregory Leeds, looking as distinguished as ever, arrived. At his side was Murray Charter, a smile fixed firmly in place.

Gregory Leeds stopped when he was halfway inside the office and looked at his daughter. He was immediately struck by the change he saw. He realized that it was not just a change in her looks, but in some indefinable way, a change in her entire being.

Her eyes met his, and he saw power and determination in them. Her deeply tanned skin looked healthier than ever, and when she stood and came around to greet him, he saw that she was dressed, not as he had expected, but in a beautiful and obviously well-tailored western dress.

"Hello, Cassandra," he said, gazing fondly at her, separated by a mere three feet.

"Hello, Father. You do remember Mr. North?"

Gregory Leeds smiled, giving his daughter a point for taking him off guard. He had been so caught up in the sight of her that he hadn't noticed the general manager.

"Mr. North," he said, nodding to Kirk for a split second before looking back at Cassandra. "You look . . . radiant, Cassie."

"Thank you, Father."

"But now," Leeds began, his voice changing as he took on his role of chairman of the board once again. "It's time for our accounting."

Cassandra smiled. "Don't bother."

"Don't bother?" her father echoed, his powerful front again slipping as a smile of victory curved the corners of his mouth. "You're conceding?" he asked, puzzled by the ease of the victory.

"No, Father, you didn't win, you lost," she stated, letting all the bitterness that filled her spill into those few words.

"Lost? Impossible. . . . Cassandra," he began, but Cassandra cut him off as she stepped back and shook her head.

"Why is it impossible, Father? Is it because you lied to me and to Kirk?"

"Cassandra," Gregory Leeds began again, but his daughter cut him off once more.

"Did you think I'm such a fool that you could manipulate me in any way you wanted? Did you forget who I am? If you did, let me remind you. I'm your daughter! Your flesh and blood! I know I've disappointed you for many years. I know that when I reached out to you, when I needed you and your love, you were nowhere to be found. But I never expected you to lie to me. To cheat me out of what I worked so hard to get.''

"Stop, Cassandra. Stop before you say something you might regret.'' Leeds turned to Kirk. "Forgive us, Kirk; this should be a private discussion. If you'll excuse us . . .''

Kirk stood still, his expression unreadable.

"No, Father. Kirk stays. He's part of this. Didn't you think we'd find out?''

"Find out what?''

"Please!'' Cassandra snapped. "Spare us your innocence. First,'' she said, holding up one stiff finger, "Carway Distributing, a wholly owned subsidiary of Leeds. When you saw my third-quarter report, you ordered Carway to drop their prices so that I couldn't make a profit!

"Two! Security clearance, five point zero. Password, *reserve*. Wonderful password; too bad it couldn't keep us out. Would you like to know exactly how much natural gas you expect to pump while you destroy the land?''

"That's enough!'' Gregory Leeds roared.

"No, sir, it's not,'' Kirk said as he stepped forward to hand the chairman of the board an envelope. "My resignation. You would have had it much sooner, but Cassandra asked me to wait until today. I dislike being used, Mr. Leeds, and being lied to.''

"And I, Father, feel the same way,'' Cassandra informed him. "Together, Kirk and I proved that Twin Rivers could turn a profit. We didn't because you wouldn't allow it. But we know we can, and we plan on doing just that.''

"Doing just what?'' Gregory Leeds asked, his eyes shifting back and forth from one to the other, his face an expressionless mask.

"Running a ranch—one that isn't a tax dodge. A ranch that won't eventually be destroyed by pumps and pipelines. You may have thought you were putting one over on me, Father, but you didn't. In the end, you lost." Cassandra paused to take a breath and then turned to gaze at Kirk, love filling her features. "Ready?" she asked in a soft voice.

"Ready," he replied, reaching out and taking her hand in his. Without another word, they walked out of the office, out of the house, and went to the Land-Rover. Just as Cassandra was about to get in, she heard her father's voice call from a few feet away.

"Where are you going?" Gregory Leeds asked, his voice level, his eyes locked on his daughter's.

"Where am I going, Father? To be married, and then wherever my husband and I decide to go."

A heavy silence filled the air and lasted until Gregory Leeds nodded his head. "Do you know what you're doing, Cassie?"

Cassandra straightened her shoulders and smiled at her father. "For the first time since I was nine, I know exactly what I'm doing."

"I see," Leeds replied dryly. Then he looked at Kirk. "And you, Kirk? Do you think you can keep her 'down on the farm'?"

Kirk pursed his lips for a moment. Then he shook his head slowly at the white-haired man. "Mr. Leeds, my father taught me a long time ago that there are only a few things in life that are certain. I know that one of the certainties is that Cassandra and I love each other deeply. The other is that there will always be horses to ride and land to live on. Good-bye, Mr. Leeds," Kirk said as he sat in the driver's seat and Cassandra sat down next to him.

"Wait. Please," he said, walking closer to the open vehicle and gazing in. "You can't just run off and get married."

Cassandra shook her head even as she took Kirk's hand in hers. "We aren't running off. We waited to tell you. Now, if you'll excuse us, we're expected at the judge's house. The wedding will take place in exactly one hour."

"I see," Leeds said as he continued to look from Kirk to Cassandra. Then he smiled disarmingly. "I know you won't believe me, but I'm glad for both of you, very glad."

"You're right," Cassandra snapped, but Kirk squeezed her hand tightly in unspoken caution.

"Cassandra, I knew that in sending you to Twin Rivers you would either be defeated or become the person you were always meant to be. Your fear of horses has held you back all your life, and I knew if you were able to conquer that fear, the world would be yours for the asking."

"I never wanted the world, Father."

"Whether you did or not, it was waiting for you."

"Under your guiding hand? Tell me, Father, if I . . . we hadn't found out about your deception until later on after everything was over, would you have forced me to keep my promise?"

"If you hadn't found out about it by now, you never would have," he replied, avoiding the heart of her question.

"But it's all rhetorical now, isn't it?"

"No, it isn't!" Leeds stated in a firm voice. "You did what you set out to do. You made yourself independent. You have a life that you've created for yourself. For that, I deserve a thank-you."

Cassandra clutched Kirk's hand even tighter. "You do, Father. Thank you." Cassandra realized as she blinked back her tears, she meant what she'd just said. She saw, too, in the depths of Gregory Leeds' eyes, he had spoken the truth as he saw it.

"Are you really going to get married?"

Cassandra stared directly at him. "Watch us, Father." Then she turned to Kirk with a smile. "Ready?"

Kirk released Cassandra's hand and started the Land-Rover. Then he looked at Cassandra. Cassandra gazed back at him with an unwavering stare. Kirk pressed the accelerator and drove away from Twin Rivers for the last time.

When the Land-Rover disappeared from view, Gregory Leeds walked back into the house. The smile on his face was a reflection of his innermost feelings.

"Greg, are you all right?" Murray Charter asked his oldest friend.

"Absolutely."

"But this marriage?"

"Kirk North is a good man," he stated. Then he shook his head slowly. "Murray, I'm going to call Eleanor and tell her she's about to become a mother-in-law. Why don't you make that phone call we discussed earlier."

The comptroller nodded his head and walked over to an empty desk, while Gregory Leeds stood still. A moment later his call was answered by the broker who handled all the Leeds stock dealings. Murray Charter spoke only a few words. The man at the other end didn't even reply.

"Finish the Barwell Industries takeover" was Murray Charter's order.

When he hung up the phone, he nodded to Gregory Leeds.

Gregory sighed. "Please find out where they're going to be married." Then he turned and went into Cassandra's office. He would tell his wife what had happened and how they had both been right when they'd decided to push their daughter into a corner to make her find some direction in her life.

And one day soon, he hoped, she would really understand his actions.

The sun graced the garden with a soft majesty that bathed the four people standing in the middle of it with a golden light.

Cassandra and Kirk held hands lightly, their eyes fixed on each other as the judge proclaimed them husband and wife.

"You may kiss the bride," he said with a warm and solemn dignity.

Kirk lowered his head, and Cassandra raised her mouth to him. Their lips met in a kiss that sealed the promises they had just spoken.

A moment later they parted, and as Cassandra and Kirk looked at Jane they saw the twin trails of tears sparkling brightly on her cheeks.

"You're supposed to be happy for us," Kirk said teasingly.

"I am. I just never thought it would happen. Do you know how close to insanity the two of you nearly drove me?"

"Not close enough," Kirk retorted.

"Thank you," Cassandra whispered as she went to Jane and embraced her.

Cassandra stiffened. Over Jane's shoulder, she saw her father standing near the house, watching them with a proud smile on his face.

"Kirk," she called.

Kirk saw that she was staring at her father. His eyes

locked with Gregory Leeds', who nodded his head once, turned, and walked away.

"Kirk?" Cassandra asked, her hand tight on his arm.

"He just wanted to watch."

Ten minutes later Kirk opened the door of the Land-Rover, and was about to help Cassandra in when he saw a Twin Rivers' envelope lying on the seat.

Reaching down, he picked it up and looked at the handwriting. It was addressed to Mr. and Mrs. Kirk North.

"What is it?" Cassandra asked.

Kirk handed her the envelope and waited for her to open it. He saw a frown crease her brow. A moment later she handed him the note from her father. Cassandra's eyes misted as she read the short statement.

My deepest wishes for a wonderful marriage. Please accept this gift to start your life together. Cassandra, you've made me very proud. I love you.

"From Father," she said in a low, surprised voice.

Kirk read the short note that Gregory Leeds had penned and then glanced at the oblong yellow slip attached to the note before looking back at his wife.

"What do you want to do about this? Do you want to accept it?" he asked as he held up the check that her father had given them as a wedding present.

"That's up to you," she said, her voice as level as possible.

"No, ma'am! This decision is all yours."

"All mine?" she asked.

Kirk handed it to her. Cassandra stared at the check. "It would more than cover the down payment on a ranch and leave us with all your savings and the money I saved from my salary.''

"That it would," Kirk replied.

"Yes, it would," Cassandra said as she lifted up the check in the amount of one-hundred-and-fifty-thousand dollars and tore it into quarters. Then, smiling back at Kirk, she flung the pieces of paper into the air and watched them scatter in the soft Arizona breeze.

"We can do it by ourselves, Mr. North," she said.

"Yes, we can, and we will, Mrs. North," Kirk replied as he drew her into his arms and kissed her deeply, passionately, and lovingly.

Silhouette Special Edition

JULY TITLES

MANDY'S SONG
Jeanne Stephens

TO LOVE A DREAMER
Ruth Langan

RENDEZVOUS
Nancy John

A WORLD OF THEIR OWN
Linda Wisdom

SILKEN THREADS
Monica Barrie

HAVEN OF TENDERNESS
Carolyn Thornton

Silhouette Special Edition

COMING NEXT MONTH

THE BLACK KNIGHT
Carole Halston

All she had to do was choose:
She could marry James Patton, the "black knight" of
her dreams, and return to the life of luxury she had
once known. But James was still jealous of Jane's late
husband. Was it love that brought him back, or was
he still trying to best an old rival?

ONE PALE, FAWN GLOVE
Linda Shaw

Madelyn Grey expected to create a stir when she
presented herself at the mansion of Owen Prince,
governor of Kentucky and candidate for U.S.
President, to announce that she was his long-lost
daughter. But she could not anticipate the reaction
of the governor's adopted son, Taylor Champion...

PLAYING THE ODDS
Nora Roberts

Win, lose or draw, Serena and Justin were meant for
each other, proving indisputably in this case that
lucky in cards did not mean unlucky in love.

Silhouette Special Edition

COMING NEXT MONTH

THE MOVIE
Patti Beckman

Kirk's biggest movie, a personal tribute to an old love, lost millions and ruined his marriage to Natalie. Now he wanted her to star in his comeback film, an adventure mystery. But, for Natalie, the real mystery was: *why* did he want her back?

THIS CHERISHED LAND
Ada Steward

Summer wanted to hate Cullen McAdams. He'd stolen Belle Terre, shattered her dreams. Instead, she fell under the spell of this cherished land, and the man who could turn a plot of Mississippi mud into a field of flowers.

BY ANY OTHER NAME
Dixie Browning

All Brianna's work seemed to be in vain when Rawls Smith appeared on the scene, claiming ownership of her home. How could they both be named owner? What was in a name? The answer to that question wasn't an easy one, but they'd work it out — for with one look, Brianna and Rawls knew that no other love could be so sweet.

Four New
Silhouette Romances
could be yours
ABSOLUTELY FREE

Did you know that Silhouette Romances are no longer available from the shops in the U.K?

Read on to discover how you could receive four brand new Silhouette Romances, **free** and **without obligation,** with this special introductory offer to the new Silhouette Reader Service.

As thousands of women who have read these books know — Silhouette Romances sweep you away into an exciting love filled world of fascination between men and women. A world filled with

age-old conflicts — love and money, ambition and guilt, jealousy and pride, even life and death.

Silhouette Romances are the latest stories written by the world's best romance writers, and they are **only** available from Silhouette Reader Service. Take out a subscription and you could receive 6 brand new titles every month, plus a newsletter bringing you all the latest information from Silhouette's New York editors. All this delivered in one exciting parcel direct to your door, with no charges for postage and packing.

And at only 95p for a book, Silhouette Romances represent the very best value in Romantic Reading.

Remember, Silhouette Romances are **only** available to subscribers, so don't miss out on this very special opportunity. Fill in the certificate below and post it today. You don't even need a stamp.

- - - - - - - - - - - - - - - - - - - ✂ - - -

FREE BOOK CERTIFICATE

To: Silhouette Reader Service, FREEPOST, P.O. Box 236, Croydon, Surrey. CR9 9EL

Readers in South Africa—write to
Silhouette Romance Club, Private Bag X3010, Randburg 2125

Yes, please send me, free and without obligation, four brand new Silhouette Romances and reserve a subscription for me If I decide to subscribe, I shall receive six brand new books every month for £5.70, post and packing free If I decide not to subscribe I shall write to you within 10 days The free books are mine to keep, whatever I decide. I understand that I may cancel my subscription at any time simply by writing to you. I am over 18 years of age. Please write in BLOCK CAPITALS

Signature _____

Name _____

Address _____

_____ Postcode _____

SEND NO MONEY — TAKE NO RISKS.
Please don't forget to include your Postcode.

Remember postcodes speed delivery Offer applies in U K only and is not valid to present subscribers Silhouette reserve the right to exercise discretion in granting membership If price changes are necessary you will be notified. Offer expires December 1985

EPS1

Silhouette Special Edition

Your chance to write back!

We'll send you details of an exciting free offer from *SILHOUETTE*, if you can help us by answering the few simple questions below.

Just fill in this questionnaire, tear it out and put it in an envelope and post today to: Silhouette Reader Survey, FREEPOST, P.O. Box 236, Croydon, Surrey CR9 9EL. You don't even need a stamp.

What is the title of the *SILHOUETTE* Special Edition you have just read?

_____

How much did you enjoy it?

Very much ☐   Quite a lot ☐   Not very much ☐

Would you buy another *SILHOUETTE* Special Edition book?

Yes ☐   Possibly ☐   No ☐

How did you discover *SILHOUETTE* Special Edition books?

Advertising ☐   A friend ☐   Seeing them on sale ☐

Elsewhere (please state) _____

How often do you read romantic fiction?

Frequently ☐   Occasionally ☐   Rarely ☐

Name (Mrs/Miss) _____

Address _____

_____

_____ Postcode _____

Age group: Under 24 ☐   25–34 ☐   35–44 ☐
                 45–55 ☐   Over 55 ☐

Silhouette Reader Service, P.O. Box 236, Croydon, Surrey CR9 9EL.

Readers in South Africa—write to:
Silhouette Romance Club,
Private Bag X3010, Randburg 2125.